Gordon S. Dickson was born not far from Inverness, Scotland, but left there soon after when the family returned to Northern Ireland. He was educated in secondary and grammar school up to 'A' Level. He was employed in the Civil Service for several years and is now retired. Venturing into writing, he has had several books published. He enjoys reading, mainly historical fiction, and watching soccer and snooker.

Gordon S. Dickson

DETECTIVE DENISON FACES RETIREMENT!

A Sequel

AUSTIN MACAULEY PUBLISHERS®

LONDON • CAMBRIDGE • NEW YORK • SHARJAH

A CIP catalogue record for this title is available from the British Library.

ISBN 9781035893393 (Paperback)
ISBN 9781035893409 (Audiobook)

www.austinmacauley.com

First Published 2025
Austin Macauley Publishers Ltd®
1 Canada Square
Canary Wharf
London
E14 5AA

With thanks to my cousin, Esme Briggs, for reading over the initial draft.

Table of Contents

Chapter 1
First Day as a Pensioner

Detective Chief Superintendent Walter Denison was only days away from retirement and becoming a pensioner. *He was looking forward to it,* I thought.

May I introduce myself? I am his successor. My name is DCS Jacob Marley and, before you ask, I am not a Dickensian character. If I had a pound for every wisecrack from smart-Alecs, I would be a millionaire! 'Seen any ghosts recently?' or 'How's Tiny Tim?' or 'Are you having a goose for Christmas?' I have heard them all, a thousand times, so don't bother.

Marley was tall, dark and handsome—at least he thought so! Actually, he did strike a fairly imposing figure for he was tall. We have to give him that. He stood just a tad under six feet three inches. His hair was dark, yes, but thinning, his eyes blue-ish, chin sort of weak, but handsome he certainly was not. Not that anyone would dare tell him so.

He had been educated at Little Worthing Private Academy, Staffordshire and King's College, Cambridge.

I had thought at one time of officially changing my name, to Jacob Marlboro or something, but it would have caused problems with police records. The guy in charge of the records section threw up his arms in horror at the thought of the problems it might cause. Not least the confusion possible to my promotion, pension etc.

Anyway, I am taking over the post here at Castlewood Police Headquarters, in the County of Staffordshire, England. I am known as Jacob, never Jake, to the folk here. Some students at Uni insisted on calling me Jake. I soon put them right, pretty quickly. (I played rugby for the First XV and did a little boxing. Enough said.)

Castlewood is a small city in east Staffordshire between Lichfield and Burton upon Trent.

Retiring DCS Denison said, as we shook hands, 'Pleased to meet you, Mr Marley. I hope you will be as happy here as I have been.'

'I hope so,' I replied, 'though I'm sure you have had your share of hairy moments, Walter. May I call you Walter? And do call me Jacob.'

'Yes, certainly, Jacob,' Denison replied. 'I think I can vaguely remember meeting you before, at some function or other.'

'No need for formalities.' I smiled. 'Yes, I think we did. Can't place it though.'

I continued, 'So far, this place seems like a nice spot to work. I was born not far away, actually.'

Denison replied, 'Yes, the staff are a good bunch. We had one bad apple some years ago. I say, "bad" but the chap was being threatened by two ne'er-do-wells called Malone and Harvey. The chap's sister had been kidnapped and he, Sol Reid if memory serves, was forced to pass on info to the pair. Both, I am glad to say, are in prison this twenty years or so. I might as well tell you now, they are due, inexplicably, for parole boards soon. I have asked the prison governors, they are in separate prisons as they hate each other, to inform you when they get out. They will no doubt return to their old haunts.

'I suspect them of being behind the gruesome murders of six informers back in the day; I was just promoted to DCI then. Six males, tortured, terribly mutilated and shot in the head. One was named Wally Mulgrew who had informed on Malone and his pal. All the others, if I remember correctly, had also snitched on them. Of course, informers informed on lots of wrong-uns so it could have been anyone who bore a grudge. The pair of them were already in prison at the time, for other murders, and I could not get enough evidence against them.

'Oops, where are my manners?' Denison changed his thread of speech. 'Would you like tea or coffee?'

'Tea, black, no sugar, will be fine, thanks,' I said.

I was fascinated by his detailed memory of such an old case. I can hardly remember what I had for breakfast. That's a joke, by the way!

Denison lifted a phone and asked for two teas, one with milk and four sugars (for Denison) and one without. Presently a detective constable brought them in two large mugs, piping hot, with a large plate of biscuits. Denison, I noticed, appeared to be fond of his food. He was, shall we say, rotund.

Denison resumed, 'As I was saying, they had murdered a young lad, George Matthews, who was due to take up a post as curate in the cathedral. Harvey then impersonated Matthews to drop out of sight, as it were. Also killed was

Billy Bowler who informed on Malone. A really gruesome murder. On top of that, they murdered two of our detectives: DS Gwen Travis and DC John Savage. That was the start of the whole episode. We think they must have stumbled on the pair's activities. Gwen and John were found dead, murdered, and their bodies thrown in the River Trent. Clues pointed to at least one of the men, Sidney Malone, as being involved. Extensive searches of here in Castlewood and in Burton upon Trent eventually led to the arrest of Malone and his crony Jake Harvey. The details are on file so I won't go into them now. It happened quite a while ago, Jacob. Twenty years or so. Doesn't time fly!' He paused for breath.

'You have a good memory, Walter. Me, I need to write everything down or I'll forget,' I said. He was obviously still much aggrieved by this case. I'm not sure it is good to be so obsessed with your work. Personally, I do try not to be.

The two murderers, Sidney Malone and Jacob Harvey had each received prison sentences of thirty years for the murders of the two detectives and others, with at least twenty served before being eligible for parole. This was while Denison was serving as a detective inspector. (read DI Denison stories). Harvey had put the blame for the murders of the two detectives on Malone to get a lighter sentence, he hoped. Malone had likewise blamed Harvey. This caused great hatred between them so they were housed in separate prisons. Their release was now possible due to parole board hearings. Both had behaved themselves in prison. At least, the governors had not heard of any misdeeds.

'Aye,' said Denison, 'but there has never been a day gone by when I have not thought about getting those two banged up for the six deaths of the informers. I am as certain as summer follows spring that those two were behind the killings. A bloke named Colin Harrison was eventually jailed for killing the six—his accomplices were not caught as he refused to name them—and I could not prove a substantial link to Malone and Harvey.

'While I have largely enjoyed the work here, I am looking forward to retirement,' Denison continued. 'She-who-must-be-obeyed, bless her, has already booked a month's Caribbean cruise on the "Aurora" out of Southampton, so there's no going back.' He chuckled which made his chins wobble! 'We leave in twelve days. Last word in luxury, apparently.'

Walter Trevor Denison was as broad as he was tall, almost. He stood five feet five inches tall in his socks. Now aged sixty-five he was as large in the waistline as ever. When purchasing a car, he had to make sure he would fit behind the wheel. His present car was over ten years old.

Denison loved his food: his wife, Millicent, was an excellent cook. 'That's why I married you,' he often joked. Millicent was unimpressed but took it in good part.

Almost completely bald now, he had dark blue eyes and large ears. When out of earshot, no pun intended, his colleagues often mentioned elephants! He sported a Clark Gable moustache since his thirties which he often declared was a hit with the ladies. His wife thought, but never said, *The only resemblance between you and Clark Gable is that you are both male.* She loved Gable's films. She had watched "Gone with the Wind" many times. It annoyed Denison when she would pre-empt the dialogue.

I replied, 'I hope you have a long and happy retirement, Walter. Give my best wishes to your missus. I remember, vaguely, meeting her, a lovely lady—Millicent, isn't it?—at that do, some years ago. Somebody's retirement I think it was.'

'Yes, Superintendent Wiggins' retirement I now recall. 'Poor chap died a few months later, unfortunately,' Denison said. 'I hope I last a bit longer.' He chuckled again.

'Well, Jacob,' Denison said, 'finish your tea and I shall show you around and introduce my staff, er, your staff, as they will be from tomorrow.'

I drained my mug of tea and munched a final biscuit. Custard creams, my favourite.

We both went round all the staff in the Murder Investigation Team, MIT as it is known, though afterwards I could remember few of the names. I gradually got to know them, of course, in time.

Back in his office, Denison continued, 'After they, Malone and Harvey, were put in prison, the six informers were also murdered as I have said. The brutality was unprecedented in my experience before, or since. They, or at least some of the victims, had informed on that pair so I have suspected they were involved in organising the murders. Oops, sorry, I'm repeating myself. Old age,' he said. I told him it didn't matter. He continued, 'The investigation was hampered by the fact they were in separate prisons. They accused each other of betrayal and hated each other. There was never enough evidence to link them to the killings, so I promised myself that if ever they were released I would hunt them down.'

'Which is where I come in,' I suggested, smiling, to stop his flow. He was obviously not going to stop talking on the subject.

'Yes, I'm afraid so, Jacob,' Denison replied. 'Of course, I will help in any way I can even though I am retired. You only need to ask.' He looked hopeful like a puppy wanting a treat.

'No doubt that could be very helpful. I'll see how things go,' I said, trying not to commit to anything. I was not sure about a retired cop working on a case. I did not want to be unkind and say I would not want his help. Us cops usually do not like retired cops interfering. I smiled and finished a second mug of tea.

Sensing I was not going further, Denison said, 'Right, I hear the staff have a farewell party prepared for me, so come along and enjoy. It will be a good opportunity for you to chat with them informally.'

'Sounds good,' I said, 'I am feeling kind of hungry. I can smell sausage rolls.' I laughed, sniffing the air.

Denison was presented with a gold watch and a wallet stuffed with cash. His staff were extremely generous. I hope I am as well thought of when I retire! Don't hold your breath, Jacob.

The next morning, I walked into my new office. It was a bit daunting I must admit, but my new staff seemed very efficient.

Six cases were requiring immediate action: three murders and three attempted murders. One of the latter was a hit-and-run where an angry wife had, allegedly, tried to kill her husband with the family Mercedes. How the other half live! Three cars, very pricy, ten bedrooms and six bathrooms mansion, swimming pool. You name it, they had it. No doubt he had left all to the wife in his Will. A motive of course!

I called the detectives into my office for an informal chat to get to know them.

They were Detective Sergeants Robin Quentin Sanderson, Kelvin Grant, Daniel Jeremi Parker (his mother was Polish hence the Jeremi, pronounced Yeremy) and Mary Sandra Freeman, and Detective Inspectors James Kavenagh and Harry Lee Trevelyan. All had worked with Denison for years. I had the immediate impression of a reliable bunch. Of course, everyone was on their best behaviour!

'Right, everyone, grab a seat.' They all sat around my desk, a large mahogany affair covered in in-trays and out-trays. The in-trays were full. The outs, as yet, empty. 'This is my first day here in Castlewood nick, though I have worked in Stoke MIT for four years. Being detectives you will know that already.' They laughed. 'I am sure we will get on famously. A good team, a band of brothers, and sister.' I smiled at Mary. They all laughed obligingly at my little jest. It is always best to laugh at the boss's jokes.

'Now, tell me a bit about yourselves. We'll start with you, Mary,' I said.

'I am from Manchester originally, sir. Got married and came here to Castlewood. My husband, Cyril, is a bank manager. We live on the edge of the city on the Lichfield road. I have been in the police for twelve years. Three in this branch,' Mary said. She was of average height with short auburn hair and brown eyes, with attractive, but not delicate, facial features. She obviously spent many hours in the gym. I later learned she played for a ladies' rugby team! Castlewood Rugby League Team, The Tigresses.

'Robin, you next,' I said.

16

Robin Sanderson spoke for the first time. He was a quietly spoken studious-looking chap. Tall with cropped black hair, clean-shaven, black-rimmed glasses. 'I have always lived in Staffordshire, sir. In the cops since I left school. It was always my dream, being a cop like my dad. In MIT for four years and love it.'

I said, 'Yes, Jim Sanderson?' Robin nodded. 'I remember working with him back in the day. Okay,' I said. 'What about you, er, Kelvin?'

Kelvin Grant said, 'Well, sir, I was born in Canada, Toronto actually. My parents came here when I was aged ten, and I joined the police when I was old enough. Like Robin, I have always wanted to be a cop. Wanted to join the Mounties, the RCMP, but we emigrated. I wish we used horses here.' We all laughed. 'Been here in Castlewood MIT four years.' He was of average height, broadly built, slightly receding hairline and with the movie star looks of actor Sidney Poitier. Ideal for a James Bond sort of character. He still had a slight Canadian accent.

I said, 'And what about you, Daniel?'

Daniel Parker cleared his throat and said, 'Much the same as the others, sir. Only, I tried working in an office, firm of accountants, for two years or so stuck behind a desk, and was thoroughly bored. Frankly, it drove me up the walls.' He chuckled. 'Applied to the police and here I am…still behind a desk, sometimes!' He grinned.

He was well over six feet tall, broad-shouldered from playing amateur cricket. He was a much-feared bowler by his opponents: many batsmen had returned to the pavilion 'out for a duck'. One memorable occasion saw three batsmen in a row bowled out. A spectator had captured it on

17

film. His, Parker's, work now made regular matches almost impossible.

He had dark hair with a reddish tinge. It merged into a neatly trimmed, ginger beard and moustache.

'Now, your turn, James,' I said.

DI James Kavenagh said, 'Sir, I have been through several branches of the service but MIT is the best. Never a dull moment, and having a good boss helps.' He grinned. He had dark hair, brown eyes and sharp features. Intelligent looking. A strong face that said, 'I'll stand no nonsense from lawbreakers'.

'And finally, Harry, is it?' I asked.

'Yes, sir, Harry Trevelyan.' He was short and stocky with fists like a blacksmith. *Handy in a scrap,* I thought. 'I started straight from school too. Have enjoyed every minute, well, nearly every minute. I like the satisfaction when a crook is locked up or an innocent person is cleared. Gives me a good feeling.'

'Hmm, don't we all?' I said and we all laughed.

'Now, where are we with the six current cases?' I asked.

James spoke before the others. 'The three attempted murder cases are in court in the next few weeks, sir. They are in your diary. Pretty straight forward; plenty of evidence so conviction is certain. Well, as certain as we can be with the juries. The woman accused of trying to kill her husband was caught on CCTV running over him twice. He is still in hospital with two broken legs and a mangled arm.

'Two of the murder cases had enough forensic evidence for arrests. The perpetrators, alleged perpetrators, were charged and now face a court. I would like more proof which is why CCTV and witnesses are being checked again.

In the third murder case of a man named Mulgrew, Fred Mulgrew, a bouncer at a local nightclub, a neighbour heard what sounded like a fight, shouting, a shot, and then silence. He looked out of a front window. Moments later, a man ran out of the house, got into the passenger side of a waiting car, then the car was driven off at speed. Obviously, there was another person in the car. The streetlights nearby were out unfortunately so the neighbour could not see the driver clearly.'

I said, 'So, you checked CCTV and speed cameras?'

'Yes, sir. Two possible vehicles have been identified in the area, speeding, and we are seeking the drivers,' James said.

'Seeking?' I queried.

'Yes, sir. One, Jack Reynolds, is reported to be abroad for the past two months, and the other has reported his car stolen.'

'When?' I asked. I already suspected the answer.

James replied, 'Er, the morning after the incident, sir.'

'Hmm, just as I thought. Have you checked his story?' I asked. 'What's his name, by the way?'

'Yes, sir. House was broken into, he claimed, and the car keys lifted. He's called Archie McCrum.'

'So, someone breaks into a house, steals a car and drives to the victim's home, commits murder, or the passenger commits murder, and presumably abandons the car!' I looked sceptical. I was sceptical. It was too easy.

'Seems that way, sir. I have doubts but hard to disprove…until we find the car,' James said.

'When was this incident?'

'Two weeks ago, sir,' Harry Trevelyan interrupted. 'McCrum described it as a dark red Ford Mondeo.'

'Okay, I assume you have checked scrap yards, rivers and canals.' I was not hopeful.

'Yes, sir, but nothing so far,' Harry replied.

'Okay, keep at it. Who was driving the other suspect car if the owner was away?' I asked.

'Turns out it was his son aged eighteen, sir,' Harry said. 'Had his girlfriend with him. He claimed he was only showing her how fast the car would go.'

'Hmm, sounds probable. We know what teenagers are like; I've two of my own. It seems we can just do him for speeding. Daddy will be pleased! Check for any connection to the victim anyway.'

'Okay, sir,' Harry said.

Chapter 2
First Day of Retirement

The newly retired Walter Denison was enjoying his first morning with the prospect of a well-deserved lie-in. The first in about fifteen years…or so he hoped.

'Ah, great to be able to stay in bed,' he said aloud and he yawned and stretched. He plumped up the pillows. 'This is the life, Walter, old chap. You should have retired years ago.'

His wife was downstairs preparing breakfast. An enticing aroma wafted up the stairs.

'Nothing to do, and all day to do it in.' He grinned and stretched, then pulled the duvet up to his chin. 'Ah, bliss.' He began to sing, badly, to himself; ♪*I'm busy doing nothing, working the whole day through, trying to find lots of things not to do. I'm busy going nowhere—isn't it just a crime? I'd like to be unhappy but…I never do have the time.*♪ He chuckled and continued humming the tune.

'Breakfast will be ready in ten minutes!' his wife called from the foot of the stairs. 'Come and get it before the cat does.'

'Okay, Dear, I'll just have a quick shower,' Denison shouted. 'So much for a lie-in,' he grumbled, heading for the bathroom. Discarding his pyjamas as he went.

In the kitchen, he sat down to eat and was forking a piece of tasty sausage towards his mouth when his missus, hands on hips, said, 'So, what will you be doing this fine day, Walter?' Work was very much implied.

He gulped and sausage in suspension, offered, 'Ah, a very good question, my Dear. I'm just planning a lazy day and enjoying life, Dearest.' He spoke more in hope than in certainty.

'No time for that. You will only get under my feet. Make a start on all the jobs you have been putting off for months. The bathroom heater—broken this six months—the lock and hinges on the shed door, mowing the lawn, pruning those laurels, they are overgrown something awful, and…'

Denison had stopped listening. *So much for a leisurely retirement. I'm never going to have a minute's peace.* 'Yes, Dear, I'll see to them all in due course. Rome wasn't built in a day.' *Nor six months, O uxorial love of my life,* he thought to himself.

'What's Rome got to do with the price of apples?' Mrs Denison asked brusquely. 'Get started while I am out shopping.' She loved Denison deeply but he did get on her nerves at times! He did have annoying habits, doing nothing being one. It was bearable when he was at work but now he would be at home every day…all day!

After a large, full English breakfast, with extra bacon, his wife drove off to do her shopping. She had her eye on a new handbag in Sadie's Ladies' Fashions' window.

'There she goes as usual, spending my hard-earned cash, Cedric,' he said and smiled. 'My pension won't last long.'

Cedric the Fourth was the family cat, a large ginger and white tomcat. Like his three predecessors of the same name, he claimed the thick burgundy rug in front of the living room fire as his own. It seemed to have a permanent cat-shaped depression in the middle. Cedric looked up at Denison when he spoke, but deciding that more food was not on offer, he laid his head down again. His tail twitched for a few moments.

'You and I are on equal terms now, Cedric, old chap,' Denison continued. 'Gentlemen of leisure, that's us. Well, until the wife returns, anyway.' He chuckled.

'What shall I really do today? Bit in the garden, tidy the garage, not that the car is ever put in it. I wonder what percentage of garages are actually used for cars, and not just for storing junk?' He chuckled. 'Needs a good clear-out that's for sure.

'I am going to have a smoke whether the present Mrs Denison approves or not, Cedric. "What the eye doesn't see the heart doesn't grieve over", as someone once said. He must have been a smoker.' Denison produced a pipe, tobacco, finest Virginian it said on the packet, and matches and proceeded to light up. Great clouds of smoke ascended. He breathed in the smoke and sighed. 'This is luxury. I should have retired years ago, Cedric. This is the life.' He put his feet up on a little stool.

His pipe smoking had decades-long been forbidden by his wife, so was undertaken when she was out of the house. He always opened a window to extract the smoke…just in case! Occasionally in the past, his pipe had mysteriously disappeared never to be seen again! 'Oh, has it? That's a pity,' his wife always said, innocently. He just bought another.

Two hours later, he suddenly felt uneasy. At first, he could not figure out why, and then it occurred to him, 'I miss work,' he groaned. 'I am not retired twenty-four hours and already I am BORED!' he shouted. 'I miss the banter and ticking people off and general goings-on in the office. Doughnuts and coffee on demand. There was always someone near the coffee machine who could be prevailed upon to bring a cup.' The cat looked up when Denison shouted bored, then he lowered his head on to his paws, yawned and went back to sleep.

'I know what I'll do,' Denison said to himself. 'In a couple of days, I will wander past the headquarters and slip in to say hello. "Hi, guys, I was just passing". Then I'll chat to Jacob and bring up the subject of those two ne'er-do-well, Harvey and Malone.' Satisfied, Denison sat back, put his feet up on the couch, also forbidden by his missus, and lit the pipe again. He felt contented.

Then the inevitable happened: the neighbouring farmer decided this was the day for slurry-spreading in a nearby field. Any country dwellers will know the resulting pong.

'Drat the man,' said Denison. 'Another pipe ruined. I'll have to close the window…in a while.' He chuckled. 'I am going to have words with Old McDonald some of these days.' Denison had always promised this but never did. He did not even know the farmer's real name so called him after the children's song character. The farmhouse was up a very long, narrow lane and Denison did not have the inclination to risk his car on the potholes or to walk it. Certainly not to walk it! The reason he did not have a dog was dogs need walks. Denison thought his legs were short enough—no point in wearing them out completely.

Cedric IV stirred, stretched and jumped on to Denison's lap and curled up.

'Oh, I am honoured, Your Majesty,' he said sarcastically. 'You don't often prefer my lap to the rug in front of the fire,' Denison muttered. 'Are you feeling unwell?' He sighed and smiled. Life was good. Soon the sound of loud snoring drifted out through the window, and it wasn't the cat.

Chapter 3
This Could Be a Feather in the
Proverbial Cap

I resumed speaking with my staff the following day.

'Right then, I'm sure Detective Chief Superintendent Denison mentioned the two men called—what's the name?—Yes, Malone and Harvey. Both are due up for parole boards next week due to government sentencing guidelines. Their sentences are only partly served, so assuming they get released as no longer a threat, as if, I want them both followed day and night. Walter Denison is convinced they orchestrated the brutal murders of six informers, back in the day. I want them nicked ASAP.'

'Yes, sir, he did mention them, often. Very often in fact. It really bugged him that he could not connect them to the crime,' said DI James Kavenagh.

DS Mary Freeman added, 'It would be a great retirement present for him, sir, if we put them away again...for another thirty years at least.'

'Or permanently,' said DS Robin Sanderson. 'Their list of crimes would fill a library.' They all nodded in agreement.

'Right,' I said, 'I'll keep an ear open for word of their parole hearings. James and Harry can take one each to check their every movement if they get out. Round-the-clock surveillance. Organise your teams.'

'Okay, sir,' they said in unison.

'Meanwhile, keep on this car-thief murderer,' I said. 'I doubt if anyone would fake stealing their own car and then go to murder someone. Of course, it may have been a fight gone wrong. An argument flares up, and someone throws a punch and then shoots. Wouldn't be the first time.'

'What if he committed the murder, had a sudden panic attack and then faked the break-in, sir?' DS Daniel Parker suggested. 'And then reported the car theft next morning.'

'That sounds like a possibility, Dan. Check out the man's background, this Archie McCrum, to see if there is any connection with the victim or other crimes,' I said. The whole thing smelt a tad fishy to me.

Two days later:

'Sir,' said Harry, knocking on the door of my room, 'we just got emails from the two prison governors…the ones holding Malone and Harvey.

I looked up from my pile of work. The in-tray was emptying, slowly. 'Yes, Harry, what's the news?' I had a gut feeling it was bad by the look on his face.

'They are both, I quote, "deemed to be no longer a threat to the public" and are getting out, sir.'

'Just as we feared. "No longer a threat"! I don't think so. Somebody has had the wool pulled over their eyes. A whole flock of sheep, and no mistake,' I replied. 'Tell the others to meet here after lunch and we will make plans.'

Harry replied, 'Mary and Kelvin are out on that McCrum case, sir.'

'Hmm, okay, as soon as they return, Harry.'

'Right, sir,' Harry closed the door. He thought, *This could be a really worthwhile case to solve. I hate unsolved crimes. A feather in the proverbial cap.*

Later that afternoon, all the detectives gathered once more in my office.

'Right, Mary and Kelvin, what have you found in the stolen car case?' I asked.

Kelvin said, 'Some good news, sir. The car, or what is left of it, has been found in the trees in the middle of a roundabout junction area on the A38. That huge roundabout built recently. Locals call it the merry-go-round.'

This was a nature reserve of about twenty or so acres encircled by the road at the junction of two major highways forming an elevated stretch surrounding the natural area. The trees were in the area lower than the roads. The reserve was subject to protected species order because of rare newts or some such creatures. Protestors had kicked up such a furore that the road developer had simply built the road junction as a giant roundabout. This satisfied all parties involved.

Kelvin continued, 'It must have been driven at speed and flew off the roadway into the trees. It was hidden from the road so was not noticed until some workmen were carrying out thinning work.'

'Any bodies found?' I asked.

'No sir, but there was some blood. We are getting DNA from it,' Kelvin replied.

'Were you able to get any fingerprints?' I asked, hopefully.

'Yes, sir, the dashboard was fairly intact and a nice set of prints was obtained where the driver had grabbed the dash, presumably to leaver himself, or herself, out through the passenger window. The car was almost on its side, the driver's side and the door was jammed.'

Mary continued, 'Strange thing, sir, the right hand appeared to have only three fingers! And a thumb, of course. The little finger was missing completely, though not due to this crash. Probably cut his hand on a broken window on the driver's side. I would guess from the size of the hand that it was definitely a male.'

'Hmm, so we only need to find a bloke with three fingers on his right hand!' I said and smiled. 'I assume the car's owner, McCrum, has all his fingers.'

'Yes, he has, sir,' Mary replied. 'We can find no connection between McCrum and the victim, sir. So he is in the clear. He has never even received a speeding ticket.'

'The case of the missing digit, Watson,' Daniel Parker joked pretending to be Sherlock Holmes with a magnifying glass. We all laughed. Daniel could be relied on to crack a joke at every opportunity.

'Okay, now about Malone and Harvey,' I continued. 'The prison governors have supplied the addresses the pair have given as their residences when released. Both with supposed relatives in the city here. They could be former criminal pals. Mary, you take the addresses and look up the voters' registers and Council Tax lists to check who lives there.'

'Will do, sir,' Mary replied.

Later, Mary returned to my office. She tapped on the door.

'Come in,' I said.

'Sir, I've found the names of the occupants of those two addresses.'

'Good, good. Who are they?'

'Malone is going to stay with a George Malone and his wife Daisy, sir, as he told the prison. At 57, Crew Lane. No criminal record for this George chap.'

'Sounds like a relative alright. Maybe just never been caught! And Harvey?' I asked.

'He's at 17, River View Terrace. The occupier is a Thomas Samuel, er, P-A-T-O-N. I don't know if that is pronounced Patton or Payton, sir.'

'I knew a Scots guy once who pronounced it "Payton" so we shall go with that,' I said.

'Thomas Paton, the suspected jewel thief, I suppose. He always managed to escape due to lack of evidence,' I continued. Mary nodded. 'Well, well. The prison authorities obviously did not do a lot of checking. Thanks, Mary. We will have to keep a particular watch on those two gentlemen,' I said with a grin.

'By the way, sir, those addresses are only a few streets apart. Could be significant, don't you think?'

'Hmm, could be, seeing as they are supposed to hate each other's guts,' I replied. 'They could have got over their disagreement. We shall keep that in mind.'

Chapter 4
Denison Pays a Visit

The newly retired Detective Chief Superintendent Denison was out for a walk—well, he had driven into town and parked in the next street to police headquarters—a walk which just happened to lead him past police headquarters. He had been retired for a whole week! I was half expecting him to show up sooner!

'Ah, Superintendent Denison, sir,' said the sergeant at reception out of habit. 'How nice to see you. You out for a walk then?'

'Oh, yes indeed, Charlie. I can call you Charlie now I am a civilian.' Denison chuckled. 'Must keep fit, you know. Good long brisk walk. Keep the old weight down.' He waved a blackthorn walking stick as proof. 'Just thought I'd pop in and say hello in passing. Is Jacob Marley in, by any chance?'

'He is, sir. Just arrived back a few minutes ago in fact. Another attempted murder! Shall I call and let him know you are here?' the sergeant asked.

'Yes, might be best. He may be too busy for a social visit,' Denison replied.

The sergeant, after a brief phone call, said, 'He said to go on up, sir. You will know the way.' He grinned. He did not add that I was not overly enthused at Denison showing up.

'I should know, after all these years,' Denison replied, grinning.

Denison made his way to my office. He took a while because everyone was asking how he was doing. 'Enjoying your retirement, sir?' and many similar questions.

I saw him coming across the main office and opened my office door. I had had the nameplate changed. Detective Chief Superintendent Jacob S. Marley, OBE it read. It looked grand. I kept wanting to polish it but resisted the temptation as being undignified.

'Well, Walter this is a surprise,' I exclaimed. I was secretly hoping he was not going to make a habit of it. 'Do come in. Some tea?'

'Yes, please. Milk, four sugars, please,' Denison said. A constable nearby did the needful.

We sat at my desk and sipped our tea. I said, 'I hope you are enjoying your retirement, Walter?'

'Yes, yes I am, Jacob. No more early rising and late nights. Keeping myself busy in the garden and so on.' He paused. 'Who am I kidding, Jacob? I am bored senseless. I wish I were still working, to be honest. It is said that sixty-five per cent of retired detectives pop their clogs within six months. Something like that anyway. I hope I last longer.'

'Bound to take a while to adjust, old chap,' I replied. 'Wish I could help, but defence solicitors would probably be complaining if a retired cop were presenting evidence.' I did not wish to encourage him in his obvious quest for inclusion in an investigation.

'Yes, I suppose so,' Denison said. He sipped his tea and sighed deeply.

I did not know what to say. There was a prolonged pause. Then, inspired, I said, 'How about you being an SSO, Special Surveillance Operative, on the Malone and Harvey case?' I had made up the title on the spur of the moment. 'Unpaid, of course, and strictly off the record,' I added quickly. 'They are out of prison. I don't know how, but the parole board, in their dubius wisdom, let them out. We have their addresses under surveillance.' I hoped he could not do too much damage doing surveillance.

'Hmm, that sounds good. It'll keep me from withering away,' Denison replied. 'The missus is complaining that I am always under her feet. Me, a nuisance! As if.' He laughed.

I laughed too. 'Well, I must get a move on, Walter. Things to do *et cetera.*' I tapped the in-tray which was piled high. 'The main thing is the murder of a bloke by a crim with a finger missing,' I said.

'Hmm, should be easy to identify,' Denison said. 'Cannot think of any local wrong-uns fitting that description though. Of course, it depends on when he lost the said digit. May not be a local, of course, or not having a criminal record.'

'Well, I'll leave you to it, Jacob. Lunch sometime, old bean?' Denison stood to leave.

'Yeah, sure,' I replied. 'Give me a few days to clear this lot.' I gestured again at the piled-high in-tray. The out-tray was filling slowly. A new secretary had yet to be appointed. The former one had also retired.

'Yes, of course,' Denison replied.

33

He wandered off to a chorus of, 'Cheerio, sir' and 'Best of luck, sir.'

When I got back to work, Mary Freeman came into my office. I told her that Denison would be keeping an eye on Malone and Harvey, informally. He knew all the local bad boys and would sniff around for gossip.

'All help gratefully received, sir,' she replied. 'Or, as a certain grocery chain says, "Every little helps".'

'Walter Denison put that pipe out this instant,' Mrs Millicent Denison shouted, hands on hips. She detested pipe smoking. Unfortunately, for Denison, she had arrived home earlier than expected.

'It helps me think, Dearest,' Denison replied, meekly. 'I have a problem, well, two problems, to sort out.'

'And what might they be? How to change your socks more than once a week, and your underpants more than once a month?' Millicent asked, sarcastically.

'Nothing wrong with my socks, Dear. Nah, serious stuff. Malone and Harvey are out of prison.'

'No! Not them again! How did they get out so soon?' she asked, looking horrified. She could foresee her husband wanting to get involved.

'Got parole, didn't they, rotten beggars!' Denison replied. 'I don't know how they swung it. Some twit saying, "they are good boys now", I dare say. They should be in for another ten years.'

His wife said, 'Well, it's not your problem, anymore. You are retired, don't forget. No need for you to worry. Let Jacob do his job. He's paid to do it.'

Denison cleared his throat nervously. 'Now, do not get angry, Dearest, but I have offered to do a bit of unofficial keeping an eye on them.'

'You what!' Steam was almost coming out of her ears. '"Unofficial keeping an eye on them". I never did hear the like of it. You and I, Walter Denison, are going on a cruise next week. I'm getting the cat into a cat kennel or whatever it's called, on Saturday. He'll not like it but too bad. No excuses, no delays for two crims. Understand?' Denison did not reply. 'Do I make myself clearly understood, Walter?' She glared at him, arms akimbo.

'Yes, Dearest. I'll withdraw the offer.' Denison knew when not to continue. *When you are already in a hole, stop digging*, he thought. *I will do it but will just keep it quiet…just as soon as we get back from this cruise. She'll never know. What the eye doesn't see et cetera.* He smiled to himself.

Chapter 5
Wish I Had a Tan Like That!

'Hmm, Walter will be enjoying his cruise by now,' I said to the staff the following week as we enjoyed a coffee break.

'Yes, he has earned it, sir,' said Harry Trevelyan. 'I'd love a cruise myself, but the wife has a phobia about boats. She had watched "Titanic"!'

'Titanic phobia?' Mary added, smiling.

'Denison's missus arranged it all. He could not wriggle out of it,' I said. We all laughed.

'Now, on to other matters. I meant to ask, who was the victim of the car-thief murder?'

Mary responded, 'He was a chap named Fred Mulgrew—'

Robin Sanderson interrupted, 'Mulgrew? That name rings a bell.'

'Yes, he is, or was, the brother of a Mulgrew, one of the six victims murdered twenty years ago,' Mary replied. 'I've been reading up on the case.'

'Yes, of course,' Robin said. 'DCI Denison mentioned him…a few dozen times!'

'So, there is a connection, possibly, with Malone and his pal,' I said. I was eager to hear more.

'They were both in prison at the time, sir,' Mary said. 'They had been locked up a few months before the six murders occurred.'

'It certainly would not stop one of them arranging it, Mary,' I replied. 'There are always ways and means for prisoners to arrange things on the outside: coded messages on the phone for example.'

'I suppose so, sir. I'll check on their visitors prior to that date. Maybe one of them has a missing finger,' Mary replied. 'I checked the computer and there is no one locally on record who is lacking a digit. The local hospitals have only one case of a finger amputation in the past five years…a twelve-year-old lad who lost a finger playing rugby. A big lad trod on it. Pretty nasty.'

'With any luck, the culprit will turn up. What about our other murder cases?' I asked. We then discussed the other outstanding murder cases.

Finally, after more than an hour, I said, 'Okay, you know what to do. Go and earn your salary,' I said with a grin.

'Good morning, Jacob,' Denison said cheerfully one morning as he entered my office.

'Morning, Walter, had a nice cruise, did you?' I sat back in my chair. This could take a while! *How would you fancy taking up bird watching in the Outer Hebrides, Walter?* I thought, a bit unkindly.

'Yes, on the whole, it was very nice, except the missus refused to let me smoke my pipe, even on deck. Said it looked out of place. I got snooty looks from some passengers. I ask you, how can a pipe be out of place?

Holmes had no problem. You would have thought I had committed a crime.' He chuckled. 'Anyway, I was glad to be home again. The sea is for the seagulls and fish as far as I am concerned, Jacob.'

'Well, it was a nice experience I'm sure. Look at your tan! Wish I had a tan like that,' I said.

'It's only on my face and arms. You wouldn't catch me in a pair of those—what do you call them?—speedos.'

I laughed inwardly. The mere thought of Walter Denison in a tiny pair of speedos with his bulk was hilarious. Like squeezing an elephant into a tutu. I refrained from commenting though.

'So, what can I do for you?' I asked.

'Give me some info on Malone and Harvey. I've got to do something, Jacob. The wife was great when I was working all day, and I had excuses to put off DIY. But now she has one hundred and one jobs for me to do. Drives me round the bend, it does.'

'Well, I can sympathise with you. My missus is the same. Clearing drains, fixing electric sockets, mowing the lawn. How I detest mowing the lawn. I had to unblock the toilet yesterday. Ugh! You can imagine the scene.'

'So here is what we have on those two. Malone is living with a cousin, George and his wife, at 57, Crew Lane, here in Castlewood. Harvey is only a stone's throw away at 17, River View Terrace owned by a Tom Paton.'

Denison gaped, 'Not Tom Paton, the jewel thief? Supposedly going straight, he is.'

I replied, 'The very one. There is no record of recent crimes so he may be going straight. Now, they could be related anyway. Harvey told the prison that Paton is his cousin. We are keeping watch. So far the two ex-cons have not been in physical contact. Their phones are being tapped, of course.'

'They were supposed to be bitter enemies which is why they were separated in different prisons. But as they are now living so close it makes one wonder,' Denison said. 'Makes you wonder if it was all a front.'

'Hmm, you are not wrong, Walter. My thought exactly. Which makes me think, are they plotting future crimes? Time will tell,' I said.

'Well, if you can fit me in for a few daytime shifts watching them, I would be grateful, Jacob,' he said. 'The missus will kick up a stink if I do nights. She'll not be happy anyway.' He laughed. 'If she finds out!'

'Should be okay. Will save the police some money. I cannot pay you as it could cause problems if we went to court. The press would use it to pour scorn on us: "Cops cannot solve a crime so have to pay a pensioner". I'll run it by the Chief Constable, anyway, Walter,' I replied. 'I'll let you know.'

'Great. I'll see you soon,' Denison replied as he left, with a spring in his step.

What have I let myself in for? I wondered. *Still, what harm can he do? Would these be famous last words?* I sighed and lifted a bulky file off the in-tray.

A few days later, Denison was sitting in his car within sight of Malone's residence. Parked in a quiet cul-de-sac to blend in. He had told his missus he was going fishing. A new rod and all the paraphernalia were on the back seat, unused. He had arranged with a local fish shop to keep one or two fresh trout for him.

An all-important flask of coffee, sandwiches, a phone, an empty plastic bottle (for emergencies!) and a camera lay on the passenger seat.

He had a three-hour shift and the regular detective had just driven off. Nosy neighbours who came sniffing around had been warned not to interfere.

'Well, Walter, old chap, this is just like when you started as a detective back in, when was it? Nineteen…Oh dear, I cannot remember it's so long ago,' Denison said to himself. 'Still, I am doing something worthwhile instead of mowing lawns. Tad chilly this morning though.' He turned the engine back on to get the heater going and blew into his hands.

The house where Malone was staying, 57, Crew Lane, was situated on the other side of a green space and a kiddies' playground. There was no sign of movement as yet. The previous detective had told him no one had entered or left that morning. It was now nine o'clock. The church bell at St Chad's chimed the hour.

'Better check I have all I need,' Denison muttered. He went through the various items.

'Note pad check. Phone check. pen check. Camera check. Sandwiches, very important check. Coffee, very, very important check. Emergency bottle, for the use of, check.' He said smiling, 'Don't want any accidents! Better make sure no neighbours are around to see, in the event of an emergency!' He chuckled.

He turned the radio on and selected a classical music channel on the BBC. He found it relaxing.

Presently, a curtain twitched in number 57 which about two or three hundred metres away. Denison was instantly alert. He lifted his camera. A face peered out and

40

scanned the area then closed the curtain. Some movement at last but he could not tell if it was Malone.

Ten minutes passed before a young lad on a bicycle approached the house. Black zip-up jacket, jeans, reversed baseball cap. He dismounted and propped the bike against the garden fence. After ringing the doorbell several times, a man opened the door. Was it Malone? Denison could not see clearly.

'Morning, Mr Smith,' the lad said in a broad local accent, 'Gotta message for yah from yer pal.' He handed over an envelope.

'Oh, that's good. Thanks, Jimmy,' said Malone, for it was indeed Denison's quarry. 'Here's a fiver for you, Jimmy. Take this message to Mr Brown.' He handed another envelope to Jimmy.

'Cor, thanks, Mr Smith,' the lad said, beaming. He took the envelope from Malone, jumped on his bike and sped off.

'Wow, five quid! Money for ol' rope, Jimmy lad,' he said to himself. He peddled like the clappers to Mr Brown's residence—none other than Jake Harvey. Harvey gave him another five pounds. Jimmy was never so wealthy in all his twelve years.

'Good show. I managed to get a clear shot of him. Hope this photo is good enough,' Denison muttered. 'Obviously paying that lad to bring messages. Malone, I'll have you and your pal in the clink if it's the last thing I do.' He rubbed his hands together with glee.

He lifted his mobile phone and called me. 'Hi, Jacob, Walter here.'

I replied, 'Good to hear from you. How are you enjoying surveillance work?'

'It's grand. Beats chores at home any day. The wife thinks I'm fishing.' He laughed.

'Anything to report?' I asked. I didn't want too much detail in case I had to fib to his wife later.

'Yes, actually there is. A young lad rode up on a bike, handed something to Malone and got paid, looks like. He was waving a banknote about. He then peddled off.'

'Hmm, interesting. They must assume we are tapping their phone. They're right!' I laughed. 'Keep up the good work, Walter.'

Denison, replied, 'I was wondering if I see the lad again maybe I should follow him?'

'Not yet. The other detectives have observed that lad and other visitors coming and going. We'll let them carry on for a few days so they feel safe. Call in here, say, on Friday. We'll get the others here to compare notes. Then we will act. Okay?' I said. I didn't want Denison to sabotage our work accidentally.

'Yes, good. I'll see you Friday. Bye,' Denison said. He sat back feeling happy. Doing something useful. His watch was nearly up, so he phoned the fishmonger to have his brace of trout ready for collection. *Best not to have too many fish being caught, though,* he thought. *Millicent might get suspicious. A few tales of the one that got away will suffice.* He chuckled. 'And the cat will love the fish. Job done!'

- **Denison had made several entries on his note pad.**
- *0900 hrs took up surveillance position*
- *O913 hrs had a cup of coffee.*

- *0935 hrs young lad on bike. Handed note to Malone. Lad received another note and cash*
- *0940 hrs phoned Jacob to report.*
- *1016 hrs delivery by Tesco mobile grocery van (might try home delivery myself)*
- *1120 hrs woman leaves house—presume Mrs Daisy Malone.*
- *1200 hrs handed over to the next shift.*

He picked up the fish at the fishmonger's, then drove to a nearby park and snoozed for an hour before returning home. He wanted to make it look like he spent a lot of time fishing.

Chapter 6
Could the Lad Be Enlisted as a Double Agent?

This pattern continued until the Friday. The detectives from the two surveillance teams and Denison gathered in my office at eleven o'clock.

'Okay, then, are we all here? Good. What have we got on the two houses?' I asked.

DI Harry Trevelyan had been volunteered by the others as spokesman. He cleared his throat.

'Well, sir, the young lad called at both houses each morning. I thought, why was he not at school? Anyway, the woman at 57, Crew Lane left each day early at around the same time. Returned six hours later, approx. Working? we wondered. It would be good to see what was in the notes the lad brought. Malone and Harvey have obviously joined forces again. Question: could the lad be enlisted as a double agent?'

Harry continued, 'Neither Malone nor Harvey, sir, have left the premises that we have seen. They could be slipping out of the back way I suppose, sir, under cover of darkness'

'That is a possibility, I agree,' I said. 'But why the notes then?'

'Good point, sir,' said Harry. 'To sum up, there is nothing to suggest a criminal plot, unless we can eyeball the contents of their notes. The kid is obviously well rewarded as our lowest denomination banknote is five pounds.'

'I agree. Harry, pull the kid over somewhere out of sight of the two houses and offer him a few quid to let you see the letters. Promise him more cash if he keeps schtum, or he will be arrested as an accomplice!'

'Will do, sir,' Harry replied, smiling. 'And I'll tell him to wear a cycle helmet in future…and to go to school, or he could end up being a cop!' We laughed.

'Okay, we shall meet again tomorrow afternoon if we get a look at these notes. Right, back to work,' I said.

Jimmy, the cyclist, did not appear for two days, then Harry stepped in front of him and raised a hand to bring him to a halt, out of sight of the two houses.

''Ere wat's your game, mister?' Jimmy cried. 'I was near into yah then. My mum told me not to speak to strangers.'

Harry showed his warrant card and introduced himself.

'I ain't done nuffin' wrong, mister,' Jimmy protested.

'We have observed you passing messages between two houses, son,' Harry said. 'The men in those two houses are criminals, and we could lift you as an accomplice. So, to avoid that we require you to let us see the contents of those messages.'

'Them messages are confi, confid, er, private like,' Jimmy said, firmly.

'And I am the law. There could even be a reward for you if we nick the pair of them.'

'Well, why didn't yer say that in the first place?' Jimmy grinned. 'How much?' He held out a grubby hand.

'That remains to be seen.' Harry took the envelope and passed it to a constable in a nearby caravan. The envelope was steamed open and the message was copied, then resealed.

'Okay, son. On your way and act natural when you hand it over,' Harry said as he handed over the letter. 'You'll get a reward when they are convicted.'

'Don't worry, copper. I shall be all cool like. Besides, they pays me five quid a time, they do.' Jimmy sped off to deliver his message. He was not going to lose five pounds a time if he could help it.

Chapter 7
The Contents of the Letter Revealed

Later, in my office, we all gathered to see what was in the intercepted message.

'Right, people, here is what was in Jimmy's message,' I said. I then unfolded the paper where the officer in the caravan had photocopied it. My jaw dropped. 'Oh!' I was stunned for a minute then, recovering my composure, I said, 'This is what it says: "I know you cops will get hold of this sooner or later, so hard cheese, it is all a setup. Just my little joke. Ha ha. And don't blame young Jimmy, he is just doing it for the money". It is signed Sid M,' I said. The detectives were all stunned and very disappointed.

'Of all the low-down tricks,' Mary said shaking her head.

'You've got to laugh though,' Daniel Parker added. Reluctantly I agreed and had a chuckle.

'Okay, guys, we start again tomorrow,' I said, when things calmed down.

'They are bound to try something else, sir,' DI Harry Trevelyan said. 'They will think we will quit now they know that we know, so they might make a mistake.'

'Yes, we should continue the surveillance from tomorrow, sir,' said DI James Kavenagh. 'They will make a mistake sooner or later.' I agreed.

Daniel Parker cleared his throat. 'Sir, will it be okay if I quit early on Friday? I have an important cricket match. The team's in the local Cricket 100 semi-finals. Castlewood Victors versus Lichfield C.C.'

'Cricket 100? What's that?' I asked, not being a cricket fan.

'It is a match limiting each team to one hundred balls, that is, bowls, sir. Have to bowl them out, if possible, within the hundred or before about an hour. Very fast-paced it is.'

'Fast-paced cricket! That's got to be an improvement. Yeah, okay, Dan, provided nothing urgent crops up,' I replied. 'And good luck.'

'All the best, mate, especially as it's against Lichfield,' said Harry Trevelyan. The others all agreed.

Then I asked, 'Are you related to that bloke Luke Parker who played for Burton Albion football team years ago?'

Daniel laughed, 'Yes, I'm his younger, more handsome, brother. I was never any good at football. Cricket's my game. Sam Curran of the Oval Invincibles is my hero.' Curran, a talented left-handed batsman and bowler, was a rising star.

'Well, well, say hello to your brother from me,' I said. 'I was a great fan of his. Shame he had to give it up 'cause of that injured knee.'

'Yes, sure. Next time I see him,' Parker replied. 'He's always travelling to lecture on football tactics.'

The next morning, two officers were on duty observing both houses. There was no sign of Jimmy though, so obviously Malone and Harvey were indeed working together and now contacting each other by other means.

Jimmy meanwhile was treating his mates to fish and chips with his earnings over the past few weeks. 'You got to laugh, ain't yah? Them coppers are as thick as two short planks,' he said. His mates all laughed. 'Two blokes, the cops say they are criminals, gave me five quid a time delivering notes. Money for ol' rope it was. Unfortunately, they has made me redu…resid…er, unemployed. And worse, I have got to go to school! They said they would tell my Da if I didn't.' His mates laughed again.

I was certain our two criminals were communicating in some way but could not figure out how. No mobile phone messages were detected. When Thomas Paton, George Malone and his wife, Daisy, left their respective homes they were followed. They never met each other nor visited the other address.

'Sir,' said Kelvin Grant one day after days of surveillance, 'this is getting us nowhere. As far as we can tell Malone and Harvey have never left the house. But it seems unlikely that they would not even go down the pub. There's something we are missing.'

'I am inclined to agree, Kelvin,' I replied. 'The Chief Constable has suggested that we are wasting too much money on this. The money we could use on something else. I'm afraid we will have to give it up. Perhaps we will just have to hope they slip up some time and give us reason to nick them.'

DI Harry Trevelyan added, 'They are bound to commit some crime sooner or later, sir. If they do, we shall nab them for sure. Even if they spat—is it spat, spitted or spit?—on the pavement, I'll have them behind bars!' He grinned.

'I've no idea, Harry. You'll need to ask a teacher,' I replied, laughing.

I later phoned Denison and told him we were calling off the pursuit, at least for the time being. He was disappointed but accepted that we had given it a good try. He said he would still poke around in the local pubs and pool halls to see if any gossip was on offer. There was usually a bloke willing to tell something for a free pint. But memories in the lawless class are long and the gruesome end of informers deterred many. 'Sorry guv, I know nuffink. More than me life's worth to grass to the cops, innit?' was the usual reply.

Weeks and months passed. Malone and Harvey met up regularly, feeling safe now the police had backed off. Old enmities were set aside and they were best pals again. The pair had indeed concluded eventually that each had put the blame on the other, so were quits.

'Jake, how about pulling a job soon? Bank, or post office or such,' Malone said to Harvey.

'Yeah, no problem, Sid. I'm bored with going straight. It's not all it is cracked up to be.' He laughed. 'And I could do with some cash in my pocket. Tom, my cousin, will help I'm sure. He used to do a bit of robbing back in the day.'

The three of them started to meet regularly, usually in their local, The King's Head, the king being Charles I who lost his, to select a target. There was a secluded snug where they could talk without being overheard.

Tom Paton was reluctant to commit to a robbery. His girlfriend had threatened to leave him if he did. 'You won't see me for dust,' was the way she put it.

Denison, who had continued doing occasional surveillance work, thought to himself, *The missus is getting suspicious with all this fishing I'm supposed to be doing. And I'm getting fed up with eating fish nearly every day. I'll have to get a better cover story.*

'Right then, Cedric,' he said to the cat, 'any bright ideas? I suppose you love the fish. Well, I am tired of them. Maybe I should take up—let me think—trainspotting or bird watching or going to the library. She would be questioning me no doubt about what books I had read. And I would have to bring some home and read them! Don't mind a bit of a read now and then, but library books? Nah, too much like hard work. Too much like school. The stuff we had to study back then was so boring. Julius Cheeser as we called him and Romeo and what'sname?' Cedric jumped up on his lap, purring.

Mrs Denison arrived home from shopping a few minutes later. 'So, is this what you call doing jobs around the house, Walter Denison? Lounging around the house watching television?'

'No indeed, Dear. I have been keeping the cat company. Poor thing was feeling neglected, weren't you, Cedric?' The cat started purring again.

'Stop talking nonsense. You have that cat as lazy as yourself.' She sniffed the air. 'Have you been smoking that pipe again?'

'Certainly not, Dearest. As if I would.' He put on a butter-wouldn't-melt-in-my-mouth expression and winked at the cat, who seemed to understand.

'The lawn needs mowing so get out there while it is dry. And no more of this fishing either. How someone can waste half the day and just catch one or two fish beats me. So, no more until all your jobs are done. Do I make myself clear?'

'Yes, Dear,' he replied. Arguing would have been a waste of time. He thought, *I hope she does not check the tackle basket which has never been used!*

Denison texted me to say he would not be doing any surveillance for a while.

I replied that that was fine. The lack of funds had stopped the whole thing anyway.

There was little more I could do on the Malone/Harvey case until they showed their hand. I decided to concentrate on tracing the three-fingered-guy. There were clear fingerprints of his right hand. Unfortunately, there was none on record which matched. I had even checked Interpol's records.

'Sir, a possible match has come in for the blood sample from the three-fingered-guy,' DS Mary Freeman said later that day.

'Oh, who is it?' I asked eagerly.

'A woman in Lichfield who narrowly missed knocking down a kid with her car. She's in hospital, sir,' Mary replied. 'She had hit a lamppost and banged her head. The kid is okay. He only received minor cuts to a knee.'

'Why is her DNA on record?' I asked.

'Sir, she was involved in an argument with another person in a pub, The George and Dragon, a year ago. It developed into a punch-up.'

'Hmm, I think we need to pay this, er, lady a visit. Which hospital's she in?' I asked.

'It's the Royal Infirmary, Lichfield, sir.'

An hour later, we arrived at the Royal to question the suspect.

'Mrs Sugden?' I asked the woman in a private ward, her head swathed in bandages.

'Yes, that's me,' she murmured. She winced with every movement. 'Oh, me poor head.'

'This is Detective Sergeant Mary Freeman and I am Detective Chief Superintendent Marley of the Staffordshire Constabulary. We would like to ask a few questions if you feel up to it?' I did not really care if she did or not.

'Oh, a superintendent! I am privileged,' she replied and winced when she chuckled. 'Been only constables so far 'cause of me accident.'

'I'm afraid this is concerning a more serious matter, Mrs Sugden,' I said.

'Oh?' she replied looking puzzled.

'Your DNA has come up as a possible match in the case of a car stolen and a killing,' Mary said.

'A killing! Like a murder?' she cried. She groaned and put a hand to her head. 'I've never killed nobody and I have not stolen no car.'

I continued, 'Nevertheless, your DNA is a close match.'

'Can't be. There must be a mistake. You may get it checked again,' she insisted.

'No mistake. It is either you or a very close relative.'

'I tell you it is not me. The only relative I have is me twin brother.'

'Yes? Who would he be?' I urged, eagerly.

'My brother, er, I don't want to get him into bother, Superintendent. He is me only kin.'

'He needs to be eliminated from our enquiries, Mrs Sugden,' I insisted. 'And you have no other relatives?' She shook her head, carefully.

'Very well,' she said. 'He is Tommy, er, Thomas Paton. He lives at 17, River View Terrace, Castlewood. My maiden name was Paton.'

Mary and I looked at each other. She wrote down the details. I tried not to show my excitement at the news.

'Okay, thank you. We shall see if we can eliminate him from our investigation. It should only be a formality.' We stood and said goodbye.

Once out of the room, Mary enthused, 'Paton! That's the bloke Jake Harvey is staying with, sir! It's too good to be true.'

'It is a good lead. Harvey was still in the clink when the car-thief murder took place, but if Paton were committing crimes back in the day, he could well be doing so still. Perhaps with Harvey and Malone!'

'Things are looking up, sir. The pot of gold at the end of the rainbow,' Mary chuckled.

'Pot? A whole gold mine, Mary, a whole gold mine. Our cup runneth over—get him in for questioning.'

The next morning, Tom Paton was shown into an interview room. He had been wakened early by police banging on his door. After quickly dressing, Paton was taken out to a car by two officers. Jake Harvey looked worried as Paton exited.

I said, 'Mr Paton, you are here voluntarily. You are not under arrest and may leave at any time.'

He replied, hands in his pockets, lounging back in his chair, 'Voluntarily? Yeah, as if. But no problem, dude. I ain't done nothing, and can I have some breakfast? I'm starving.'

I ignored his food shortage. 'You have a certain person, namely Jake Harvey, residing with you. Is that correct?'

'Yeah, so what? He's my cousin and out on parole'

'To the best of your knowledge has he been involved in, or planned any criminal activity, since he was released?'

'Nope. He has been lounging around my house watching TV and eating me out of house and home. Must not have fed him in the nick.' He laughed.

I changed tack. 'Your sister Mrs Sugden's DNA has come up as a possible match in the case of a car stolen and a killing.'

'What?!' Paton sat forward sharply, his face reddened. 'No way! My sister never done no killing. She gets a neighbour to remove a spider rather than kill it. You got your facts wrong, copper.'

'She is your twin, is she not?' I asked, forcefully.

'Yeah, we are twins, but not identical obviously. I being male and she female. I'm sure you have noticed,' he said sarcastically.

'Which means your DNAs are close to identical. So, if the DNA we found in a stolen car is not hers…?'

Paton said, 'It is not mine either. I never stole no cars. I would not know how. I have never committed any crimes.'

(I thought, *He could have added that he had never been charged due to lack of evidence.*) He folded his arms defiantly. 'And I never killed nobody either, before you ask.'

I said, 'To settle the matter, we need a DNA sample from you now.'

'Yeah, okay. Knock yourself out, copper. You're wasting your time.'

I noted that he looked worried or puzzled. It was difficult to tell.

A constable came in and took a saliva sample from Paton. 'Mark that urgent, Geoff, please,' I said to him.

'Yes, sir,' he replied.

'Now, Mr Paton, you may go. We shall notify you when we receive the result. Don't leave the country,' I said.

He grunted and grumbled as he left. He took his hands out of his pockets. I noted that he had all his fingers intact so I had the feeling we had the wrong person. He could count to ten without using his toes!

Chapter 8
The Post Office Job

Harvey said to Malone and Paton, 'I'm bored sitting around the house all day. Can't we pull a job, a post office or something?'

'Wouldn't do any harm, I suppose,' Malone replied. 'The cops seem to have given up their surveillance. I remember that bank job we did in Burton back in the day. We used a staged riot at the football ground to distract the police. Great, that was. Wouldn't like to get out of practice.' He laughed.

Paton, and Jake Harvey, had not mentioned his interview with the police. He said, 'You are not wrong, Sid. You are not wrong. There's a post office on the edge of town. Nick a car, pull up outside the post office, one of us keeps the engine running, the others in and out pretty sharpish, drive off, dump the car, easy peasy. What d'you say?'

'Sounds good. We should wait until all the olds are collecting their pensions…loads of cash just for the taking. How about Thursday?' Harvey said.

'Thursday it is. Let's go and scout around it today. Familiarise ourselves with escape routes and such,' Malone added.

And so, the three of them took a bus to Nottingham Road Post Office. Denison, who happened to be on watch, followed the bus. He had decided to keep watching, occasionally, even though the police had officially let the case lie.

'Hmm, I wonder where they are off to?' Denison muttered to himself. He followed for about twenty minutes. 'Looks like they are going out of town—Just a minute! They are alighting on this road. I wonder why.' He pulled his car into the kerb behind a van so he could see and not be seen.

Malone and pals got off the bus and casually walked past the post office. It was quite quiet, being a Tuesday.

'Not much happening in there, Tom,' Harvey said. 'Is it worth knocking over, do you think?'

Paton said, 'Just you wait 'til Thursday. It will be heaving with the olds collecting their pensions. I saw them about six months ago. Droves of old dears with full purses. I have kept this place in mind ever since.' He tapped the side of his head. 'That's why I have never been nicked. They can never remember me to give a description or are too shocked to remember anything.'

'Okay. Let's take a look at the roads from here,' Malone said. 'Which is the best for a quick getaway?'

There were three routes: the road out of town to Nottingham, the return route back into Castlewood centre, and a suburban road which was through a quiet residential area. It eventually would get them back to base away from cops possibly heading to the post office. The three decided that the third was their best option.

Denison was watching all this. 'Looks like they are casing that post office if I am not mistaken. And planning an escape route too. Play this right, Walter, and we could nab them all red-handed.' He said to himself, 'I really must stop talking to myself.'

He returned home and phoned me. 'Jacob, I've just seen Malone and his pals, Harvey and Paton, casing a post office for a job. I reckon they will try it on Thursday, the busiest day of the week.'

'Excellent work, Walter. Give me the details,' I replied. I wrote down the location and likely escape routes. 'By the way, Walter, we have discovered that Paton is not the three-fingered-guy we want for murder. His DNA is a close match but he has all his fingers intact.'

'Oh!' Denison replied. 'That means we can't nab him for both robbery and murder!' Denison replied. 'But it does mean that the three-fingered-guy is a relative of Paton. I had hoped maybe we could even connect Malone and Harvey with the murder. They obviously know each other.'

'With any luck, we might yet if we can get Paton to squeal. But they were still in prison at the time.' I rang off. I briefed the team and we waited patiently for Thursday to arrive.

As soon as the post office opened on Thursday morning, three unmarked police cars were sited in the surrounding roads. They waited and waited. Every three hours, new teams replaced them. I was on the three to closing time shift that afternoon. Not a sign of the robbers.

At five o'clock, I called it off. 'Okay, guys, we may as well call it off. It's a no-show. Return to headquarters,' I said over the radio.

Earlier that day, the three would-be robbers had looked out at the rain. It was coming down in stair rods.

'I'm not traipsing about in that,' said Paton. 'We will be soaked looking for a car to, er, borrow.'

'Yeah, it can wait till another day. Besides, there's a rugby international in the tele in half an hour,' Malone said. 'New Zealand v. England.'

'Put the kettle on, somebody,' Harvey added. 'I like a spot of rugger, as they say in posh schools.'

'Even better,' said Malone, 'I've a bottle of scotch, Glen Dhornoch Single Malt Whisky, I've saved for such an occasion.'

'Jolly good show, old chum, what?' Paton said mimicking a posh accent. 'Cheers!'

'Cheers!' the others repeated together.

'That was a day wasted,' I said to the team. 'Either we picked the wrong day or the gang called it off. Denison was certain they were going to hit that place.'

'There's going to be questions asked about the cost, sir,' Mary said.

'Don't remind me. I'll have to find a good excuse,' I replied. 'I'll not mention Denison…it was a tip-off from an informant if anyone asks.'

Denison decided to avoid the police headquarters for a while. He felt totally responsible for the fiasco. He had never felt so depressed.

Chapter 9
Malone Meets Denison

A week passed and Denison decided he would park and observe the post office again. Just to pass the time and avoid jobs at home! The Thursday customers were soon arriving. A Securicor van had delivered the cash needed.

Denison had his usual supply of food and coffee. He wore a wide-brimmed hat as a disguise. The hours passed but nothing happened. It was a warm day and Denison began to feel drowsy. Then suddenly, when he was about to give up and go home, there was a tap on the passenger-side window. He was startled for a few seconds until he looked over. A grinning Malone waved at him, cheekily. Hiding his anger, Denison lowered the passenger window.

'Well, well, if it isn't my old chum Detective Denison. I thought you had retired, or even better, died!' Malone said, snidely. 'Love the hat, by the way.'

Quickly recovering from his surprise, Denison replied, 'Yes, Malone, I have retired. I am just observing human nature. There are a lot of nasty people around, as you will know, being one of 'em.'

'Oh, now, now, former Detective Denison, no need for that. I am going straight as they say. Nasty things like robbing post offices do not cross my mind.' *Well, not often,* he thought. He nodded towards the post office.

'Where's your pal Harvey? Is he not with you?' Denison asked as he glanced around at parked vehicles.

'Oh, he's in a car back there.' Malone nodded towards his right. 'We are just out for a little drive…getting some air…shooting the breeze, so to speak, and we noticed our old friend Denison parked, so I thought I would say hello. Just to be mannerly, like.' He smiled innocently.

'Hmm, a likely story,' Denison said. 'Well, be on your way, Malone. Say hello to Harvey. I shall no doubt see you both heading back to prison…soon.'

'Oh dear, we are in a mood, aren't we?' Malone tut-tutted and went back to his car, a Seat Toledo he had borrowed earlier.

Denison did a U-turn, passed the other car, and noticed a third man in it, whom he recognised as Tom Paton. Paton had been of interest before but had never been caught.

To Harvey and Paton, Malone said, 'Denison has somehow sussed we were planning a robbery, lads. We might as well forget this job. There might be other cops around.'

'Of course there'll be other jobs,' Paton replied. *Just as long as my girlfriend doesn't find out,* he thought. He started the engine and drove off in the opposite direction to Denison.

Denison was furious with himself as he drove home. If only he had concealed himself better and not let Malone spot him. 'He knows my car now. Drat the man,' Denison shouted. Then he looked around sheepishly in case someone had heard him. He closed the car window.

He stormed into the house and sat down in the living room. His missus was out shopping as usual. There was a note on the hall table: "Gone shopping. Make your own dinner".

'Typical,' he grunted. He lit a pipe regardless of her disapproval. He was in no mood for being pipeless. Even the cat sensed his temper and stayed well clear. Cedric decided to do a patrol of his territory, the garden, to warn off any other moggies who just might have the inclination to scoff his dinner.

Denison muttered to himself, 'There has got to be a connection between the driver of the stolen car and the subsequent killing, and that Paton fella. Jacob says Paton's DNA test was not an exact match, and his sister's is the same. What are we missing here?' He drummed his fingers on the arm of the chair. He lit another pipe. He was having difficulty keeping it burning. 'They both said they had no other siblings. Could there be another close relative? But that would put Paton and also Malone and Harvey in the clear. I am certain they are involved. I'll prove it or die trying.

'This Fred Mulgrew who was murdered? Why? Could it be connected to the other Mulgrew who was one of the six informers killed twenty years ago? If so, why kill him all these years later? I do not recall a Fred Mulgrew being involved in any crimes or informing. Think, Walter, think. What is the link?' He tapped the side of his head.

Just then, Millicent, his wife came in through the front door. She stopped mid-stride and sniffed. 'Walter Denison, are you smoking that smelly old pipe?'

'Yes...I...am,' Denison stated in a tone which forbade any objection.

Millicent was taken aback. Walter had never spoken like that before. 'What is the matter, Dear? You sound troubled.'

'Malone and Harvey are the trouble. I just cannot get a lead to connect them to a murder case. I feel it in my gut that they are responsible in some way,' Denison answered. 'Sorry, if I was a tad abrupt just now, Dear.'

'No matter,' she said. 'I'll make some dinner and you can tell me all about them. Two heads are better than one.' She headed to the kitchen. Moments later, the microwave could be heard. Two frozen chicken dinners heating.

Sensing a pleasanter atmosphere, Cedric IV, having come indoors via the cat flap, had settled down on the rug, his favourite spot.

Denison started to relate events to his wife as they ate from trays on their laps. He had extinguished his pipe and sprayed air freshener. 'Well, as you know that pair are free. How they got parole is a mystery but we are where we are. Anyway, I suspected they were involved somehow in a murder, possibly by a bloke called Paton. This murder was of a man, Mulgrew, who was, I think, related to one of six informers killed way back. I, as you know, tried to tie those murders to Malone and Harvey. Now, because of this link, I am more convinced than ever that they are guilty. I was watching a post office—'

'You were what, Walter?' his wife interjected. 'You told me you were going fishing!'

64

'Er, I'm sorry but that was a tiny lie. I knew you would not agree to me working unofficially on the case.'

'A very big lie, Walter Denison. I suspected something was going on. You were working unofficially?' His wife was furious but tried very hard to remain calm.

'Well, yes. To tell the truth, I was bored silly being at home. I missed work. I know that sounds odd as most people are glad to retire, but my work was my life, present company excepted, and I just needed the buzz from doing something.'

'And Jacob agreed to this?' she asked, shaking her head. *I'll have words with him next time I see him,* she thought.

'Yes, reluctantly, I think. He said it could be okay if it was unpaid and off the record—but back to the post office. I was watching it this morning as we suspected the three of them were planning a raid on it. There I was in my car observing the comings and goings when Malone tapped the car window. Gave me quite a start. He seemed to enjoy the idea of thwarting my attempt to catch them in the act. So, I am back to square one but more determined than ever to nail them.

'We found DNA evidence in the car the killer, a guy with a missing finger, used when he murdered that bloke I mentioned. It was a close match to that of a Mrs Sugden. She turned out to be the twin sister of Paton, but his DNA is not an exact match either. Therefore, Jacob concluded that the murderer was a close relative. They both deny having another sibling so, again, I am stuck. By the way, Paton is not the missing-finger-guy who drove the stolen car. We have still to trace him.'

'And I suppose there are no crims on record as having a missing finger?' she asked.

'None, but of course, it could have been lost recently. The other fingerprints are not on record either.'

'Another thought: could the murderer be female? And could there have been more than one person in the car?'

'I suppose it could be a woman but a witness said he heard a fight, and the victim was a large man. I doubt many women could have overpowered and killed him,' Denison said. 'Besides, I'm told the handprint is quite large, like a man's.'

He continued, 'There certainly could have been two in the car, the driver and the killer. I'll check what the witness said. Any other prints and hairs found in the car were from the owner, Mr Archie McCrum.'

'Could this McCrum be the murderer along with missing-finger-guy? I assume he has all his fingers.'

'Unfortunately, yes, he has the normal quota of fingers,' replied Denison. 'If he were with someone, why would he use his own car, kill someone, crash the car deliberately or accidentally, and then report it stolen, after faking a theft? Besides, he would have been driving his own car and, as I said, he has his quota of fingers.'

'Yes, I see the point. It would have been more sensible to have stolen a car. Still, who says a criminal has to be sensible?' She chuckled.

'Any more tea in the pot?' Denison asked. 'I would get it myself but the cat is sleeping on my lap.' Denison grinned. The cat had jumped onto his lap as soon as Denison had removed his tray.

'Hmm, that cat has become another excuse for doing nothing,' she said laughing.

'I'll just have to hope the three of them make a mistake soon, or that missing-finger-guy will turn up,' Denison said wistfully and helped himself to a biscuit.

Cedric started purring.

Chapter 10
I Have Just Had a Marvellous Dream

We met in my office to discuss the Fred Mulgrew murder case.

I said, 'Right guys, the Chief Constable is being pressured by the newspapers about this murder. Basically, why have we made no arrests?'

'What forensics we have, sir, are not sufficient to charge anyone,' said DI Trevelyan. 'The blood DNA is similar but not identical to Paton and his twin sister, as you know, so there logically must be a sibling.'

'Logically, yes, but both say they have no other family. The neighbours of their parental home have only ever seen the twins,' said DS Mary Freeman.

'Unless a parent was playing away, so to speak,' DS Kelvin Grant added. 'It would have to be their father as the mother's pregnancy would be a bit obvious.'

'Good point,' I said. 'Let's follow that up. How, I don't know, because the local hospital, if born locally, would be unlikely to have the father's name on record.'

'Unless the name "Paton" was put on the birth certificate it will not be available that way either,' DS Robin Sanderson said. 'I'll check it out just in case. I'll go back about forty years.'

'Okay,' I said. 'We'll leave it there for the moment. Thanks. Guys.

'Oh, by the way, Dan, how did your cricket match go?'

'We lost by five runs,' Daniel Parker replied glumly. 'Our last batsman was bowled out for a duck; otherwise, we could have beaten them.'

'Who was your last man?' I asked. I suspected the answer.

'Alas, 'twas I,' said Parker being dramatic, striking a pose. 'If I had knocked one into the stands for a six, we would have won.'

'Oh, that's too bad. Better luck next time. Okay, good night all,' I said, stifling a laugh.

Denison appeared in my office a few days later, as expected. I let him know that we were still pursuing Paton as a possible suspect. He seemed to be depressed by the lack of evidence to catch Malone and Harvey. It was really bugging him. I tried to persuade him to let it go and get on with his retirement. He seemed to take that on board and wandered off after we had a quick lunch together.

Denison was still thinking about how Malone and Harvey, being with Paton at the post office, must point to them being involved in the murder of Fred Mulgrew. Mulgrew who was a brother of the Wally Mulgrew murdered twenty years before as an informer.

'There has got to be a way of proving it,' he muttered to himself as he mowed the lawn at the back of his house. His wife's nagging had finally forced him into action. 'My brain tells me they are guilty but I just cannot hit on a clue.

'Ah well, this is good exercise anyway. My gut is getting out of hand.' He patted his belly where the shirt buttons were strained to their limit. 'I'll sleep on it.'

A few nights later, at three o'clock in the early hours, he suddenly sat up in bed, wide awake. He had had a very vivid dream. Aloud, he said, 'That's it! The very man who will know if anyone does!'

'Eh? What?' his wife uttered, still half asleep. 'What are you on about? It's the middle of the night, Walter. Go…To…Sleep!' she said, angrily.

'Dearest, I have just had the most marvellous dream.'

'That's nice. Now go to sleep,' she replied, yawning.

'You don't understand. Colin Harrison, who was the only one locked up for the murders of the six informers, is still in prison. He knew a victim, Wally Mulgrew, therefore most likely, Fred Mulgrew the man killed by missing-finger-guy, and therefore probably knew Malone and/or Harvey. So, he probably knew Paton as well.' The words tumbled out of his mouth excitedly.

'So what?' She yawned again.

'So, if I can get Harrison to talk, I can get Malone, Harvey, three-finger-guy, and Paton banged up for the six killings and this latest killing. Four birds with one stone. I am going to visit Harrison.'

'Do you not think your officers back then would have questioned him about that? If he did not talk then, is he likely to talk now?' his wife asked. She had given up on getting back to sleep.

'Quite possibly, but after twenty years to think about it and that pair out free, he just may be more cooperative, Dear'

'Hmm, if you think so, phone the prison in the morning…now, go back to sleep!' said his wife. She turned over and pulled the duvet up around her shoulders.

Minutes later, Denison was snoring, loudly. Millicent groaned and put a pillow over her ears.

Chapter 11
I Need to Ask a Favour

Next morning, Denison phoned the prison where Colin Harrison was being held. Denison knew the governor from many years before. They had attended the same grammar school—the old boys' network.

'Hello, Albert, Walter Denison here.'

'Oh, hello, Walter, *longe invisus es,* long time, no see. How have you been?' the governor replied wondering what he might want. Denison recalled that Albert was a Latin fanatic. He was always top of the class. Also in French and German.

'I am fine thanks, Albert. I need to ask a favour.' Denison crossed his fingers.

'That's good. I'll do what I can of course. What's the favour?' the governor said, mystified.

'You have a lifer there named Colin Harrison,' Denison said. 'I need to speak to him, that is if he agrees, of course. Could I call to see you today, if possible?'

'Hmm, I'll check my diary, hold on a second.' He flicked through the diary. Denison heard the pages flicking. 'Yes. Walter, I have a slot at one thirty. Will that suit?'

'Yes, excellent,' Denison replied.

The governor continued, 'Tell you what, come for twelve and we'll have a spot of luncheon. There is a great little restaurant nearby. A four-star. Why not meet me there? It's called *La Parisienne*, good French cooking, and you don't have to eat snails. On expenses, of course.'

'Okay, sounds just like it's built for me,' Denison said, laughing. *And I'm not, definitely not, eating snails*, *or frogs' legs*, he thought.

'Right, see you at noon. Must go, *valeas,* bye.'

Denison turned to his wife. 'That's it arranged. We are meeting at twelve, and hopefully, we can get the ball rolling.'

'Oh, I do hope so, Dear. It will be a relief to have those horrid men behind bars again,' Millicent replied. *And an end to this obsession,* she thought. She hoped.

At noon, Denison parked in the carpark behind the restaurant. The governor had walked the few metres from the prison. He appeared at the rear entrance and waved to Denison. Denison waved back and walked to the entrance. The longest distance he had walked in a week. They shook hands.

'So good to see you again, Walter. Been too long,' Governor Albert Wood said.

'Good to see you too, Albert. Yes, must be a couple of years,' replied Denison.

'More like ten. I've taken the liberty of ordering a couple of steaks. I hope that is okay?' Wood said.

'Oh, yes, that is fine. I am partial to a nice steak.' Denison patted his stomach. Wood chuckled.

'Me too. The wife has me on a diet,' the governor said.

They went inside to a table in a quiet corner. There was a "RESERVED" notice on it. Wood signalled to a waiter.

'Joseph, a nice bottle of red to go with our steaks, please.'

'Yes, certainly, Mr Wood. I know your taste. I'll get a good vintage—French or Italian?' the waiter asked.

'French, of course. Sounds like just the ticket, Joseph. Thank you,' said Wood.

When the waiter had gone, Denison said, 'I'm driving so I shall go easy on the wine, if you don't mind.'

'No problem, Walter. I'm not, so I shall drink what's left,' Wood replied with a laugh. 'I'm taking the afternoon off. My appointments have been postponed and a taxi booked. To be honest, it is too nice a day to be indoors.'

'I cannot disagree with that. I am actually retired now, you know,' said Denison.

'Oh, yes, of course. I am retiring soon myself,' said Wood. 'I can't wait. Round of golf every day!'

'Oh, here come our steaks,' said Denison. His mouth was watering. He did not wish to be invited to play golf.

The waiter served the steaks on large oval plates. Heaped quantities of vegetables were added. Denison thought his birthday, Christmas and New Year had all arrived at once! His wife had him on a diet.

'This looks perfect,' he said as he spread a napkin over his ample lap. 'I don't often get the chance to eat so well. The missus wants me to diet too. Ugh.'

Wood laughed. 'Better make the most of it, my friend. How is your wife, by the way?'

'Yes, Millicent is very well, thank you. Still trying to stop me smoking my pipe and to mow the lawn. I shall tell her you were asking—Oh, nice,' Denison exclaimed as he sliced a piece of the steak. He chewed for a few minutes then sighed, 'Absolutely exquisite, Albert. Never tasted better.'

'Good, good. Glad you like the steak. The chef, François, knows what I like,' Wood said. 'Rumour has it he is actually Frank Bridger from Barnsley, but François Du Pont sounds better.'

Denison had a mouthful of potato and carrots so could only nod. Then he said, 'Perhaps I should speak of the reason I am here. It is about that chap Colin Harrison.'

Wood paused in his chewing and swallowed. 'Yes, a lifer. I doubt if you will get much assistance from him. He has never said a word about who was with him doing those murders'

'Yes, I thought that, but I must try. There are two crims whom I always suspected arranged the murders of the six informers, from their cells. So they must have worked with Harrison. He did not act alone, that is certain. I shall not rest while they are free.'

'But as you are retired now, why are you still pursuing this, old chap?' Wood asked. He thought it rather strange for Denison to be involved.

'Difficult to put into words, Albert. I cannot rest while only one person is convicted for those ghastly killings. The worst I have ever seen.' Denison shook his head slowly and shuddered at the memory.

'I recall the newspaper headlines. Well, let us head to the prison, when we finish eating of course, and see how he reacts. I had better not drink any more wine.' Wood chuckled and ordered some coffee.

The governor quickly arranged for Harrison to be brought to an interview room. Harrison, of course, was reluctant to do so when he heard it was Denison who wanted to meet.

Governor Wood said, 'Colin Harrison, I believe you know DCS Denison?'

Harrison glowered at them both. 'Yeah, I remember him. He got me locked up for life, he did. How could I forget?'

Denison took a seat and indicated for Harrison to sit. 'You were caught fair and square so you can only blame yourself. They were multiple murders of a diabolical nature, but I am here on a slightly different quest.'

Wood moved to the door. 'I'll leave you to it, Walter. Maybe best I am not present. Call me sometime. There is a guard just outside the door, should you need him.'

'Yeah sure, and thanks,' Denison said. Wood left.

'Right then, er, Colin. May I call you Colin?'

'Call me whatever you like, as long as it is not too early in the morning!' Harrison quipped. Denison laughed, just to be friendly. It was a rather tired, old joke.

'Okay, well, I wish to speak about two old friends of yours, namely Malone and Harvey.'

'What makes you think we are friends…Walter?' Harrison grinned.

Denison ignored the familiarity and said, 'The six men you murdered twenty years ago had allegedly informed on that pair. So, one can see a connection between you and them. One victim was named Mulgrew and a Fred Mulgrew, a brother, was murdered recently in Castlewood. I don't believe in coincidences.'

'Oh, well, one cannot see any connection, can one?' Harrison mocked, speaking posh. Denison ignored the comment.

'Why else would you have picked those six? You and your gang. You could also name them as well while I am here.'

'Leave it out, Walter, leave it out. They, if they exist, may have mates in here. Where would that leave me? Anyway, what's in it for me if I fingered Malone and his pal? By the way, they were both in clink at the time and I had no contact with them. I assume they are both still in jail.'

'They got out a few weeks ago, for good behaviour,' Denison said.

Harrison doubled over with laughter. 'Good behaviour? That pair! You have got to be kidding!'

'So, you do know them?' Denison raised an eyebrow.

'Knew them, way back. Not seen or heard from them since. Not since they were locked up. Never contacted them and they never contacted me. I definitely have done nothing for nobody as regards arranging killings.'

'They could have conveyed messages to your gang outside. Arranged for someone to put out a contract on the six and on this Mulgrew chap.'

'No way, Walter. My relatives have to force themselves to even come here, never mind convey messages. Sorry, but I cannot help you...even if I wanted to, which I don't.' Harrison sat back and folded his arms. 'No way.'

Denison hid his disappointment and said hopefully, 'The governor told me you were up for parole soon. I could have a word on your behalf with the panel. I know most of them. What do you think of that?'

'Sounds mighty nice, Walter, but I just do not know anything which might help you.' He smirked.

'If Malone and Harvey were behind the six killings, is it fair that they are free while you, Colin, are locked up possibly for your natural?' Denison had his fingers mentally crossed hoping he could get through to him.

'Well, I'll need to think about it, Walter. Give me a few days, eh?' Harrison grinned.

'Very well. I'll contact the governor in, say, a week?' Denison said, hopefully.

'Yeah, a week. And I'm going to need protection when or if I get out. New identity and stuff.'

'I shall enquire about that with the new DCS to see if that is a possibility,' Denison replied. 'I'll see you in a week.' He then left.

When he got back to his car, he breathed a sigh of relief. 'From what he said, it seems that Malone and Harvey were definitely behind the murders,' he said to himself. 'You are on to a winner, Walter, lad, just as long as he is not just stringing me along.' He looked worried.

The next morning, Denison called with me at police HQ. I could hardly believe what he related.

'Good morning, Jacob,' Denison said, cheerfully. 'I have been to visit Colin Harrison in Lichfield Gaol.'

My mouth dropped open but I quickly recovered. 'You what? You spoke to that guy? What did he have to say? I cannot believe he would be helpful in any way. The man is an animal. I have read up on the case of the six murders and it is not pleasant reading. "Madman" Harrison he was known as.'

'I am surprised too, Jacob. He has not actually said yes but wants to think about it. He has a lot to lose, namely his life if he grasses on his accomplices and Malone and Harvey. I am returning in a week.'

'I am almost speechless, Walter,' I replied. 'It will be great to get the whole lot of them behind bars. I suppose Harrison wants a change of identity if he is released. I assume he wants a favourable parole hearing?'

'Yes,' Denison replied. 'I told him I would speak to the panel. There is no guarantee they will take it on board, but it is all I could offer.'

'Hmm, there is nothing else we can do until you see him again—Cup of tea and doughnuts? I'm sure the others will want to say hello,' I said.

'Yes, that would be much appreciated,' Denison replied. Denison never refused food!

Chapter 12
Where're the Hedge Clippers?

The week passed very slowly in Denison's estimation. Patience was a virtue he lacked.

He was still looking for information on the man with three fingers, but no one had heard of one or were not saying. He could understand any informers being scared stiff of being fingered (no pun intended) by the gang who had killed the six informers. People have long memories, especially in the criminal world.

Denison was getting really frustrated. He felt like grabbing the person he was speaking to and wringing the truth out of them.

His wife had almost given up hope of him doing any of the tasks around the house. He just sat thinking, that is when he actually came home at all.

Finally, one day she said angrily, 'Walter, you have got to stop this obsession with those two criminals. It's not doing your health any good I'm sure. Look at you…no sleep, bags under your eyes, no energy. Enough is enough.'

Denison sighed. 'Yes, you are right. If this meeting with Harrison results in nothing new, I shall leave the whole lot to Jacob Marley.

'Now, I think I shall have a go at the laurel bushes. Where're the hedge clippers?'

'They are in the shed. Probably need oiled, I'm sure, as they have not been used in years,' his wife replied, sounding grim. She stifled a smile of triumph. Finally, he was going to do something.

The day of the meeting dawned. Denison was up and about early. He mentally rehearsed the answers to questions that Harrison might ask. Anything about the parole hearing, if one were likely to happen, would have to be non-committal. He had to be careful not to promise anything definite.

Arriving at the prison, the governor met him at the entrance. They had an informal chat about the procedures to be followed. The governor emphasised the importance of not committing anyone to grant a parole hearing, much less backing Harrison on it. The severity of Harrison's sentence was due to the appalling nature of the crime. Even seasoned forensic officers were sickened by it. It took days to match the severed fingers and ears to the six corpses.

Denison said as Harrison was admitted to the interview room, 'Good morning, Colin. Please take a seat.'

'Where to?' Harrison joked. He sat back looking smug. He had an unpleasant-looking face: eyes too close together, a large square jaw, overly large mouth, thick black eyebrows and a huge nose. It appeared to have been broken at some time.

'Hmm, yes, awfully funny,' said Denison, not amused. 'Have you thought about and come to a decision on the discussion we had?'

'Yes, of course I have, but what do I get out of it? I mean, if the blokes in here found out, I'm as good as dead. A knife in the back!' Harrison looked extremely worried. He had good reason to be.

'Well, of course we would keep it strictly confidential,' Denison said trying to sound sincere. He knew that there was always a possibility of a leak.

'And what if the blokes I am alleged to have had as accomplices go to court, will your source still be secret?'

'I am sure the judge would permit your name be kept out of it. In the circumstances, it is only reasonable,' said Denison. 'Witnesses are often behind screens.'

'But the supposed accomplices would suspect me. And Malone and Harvey, if they were involved with this recent killing, would also suspect me.' Harrison folded his arms and looked grim.

He continued, 'Anyway, how could I have arranged the killing of that chap, what's name?…Mulgrew when I am in here? I am sure you have checked my visitors list.'

'It has happened before. I am sure you could have devised a way,' Denison replied. 'But we need names. No one could have murdered and mutilated six men on their own. You were the only person convicted of the crime.'

'Okay, just for the sake of argument, if I gave you names, can you get me out on parole and give me a new identity? That is the very least you could do.' Harrison looked expectantly at Denison. He continued, 'Malone and Harvey were behind the six killings albeit from prison. They had fingered Wally Mulgrew instead of Fred by mistake and only found out a few months ago. So, they had Fred done too. They, Malone and Harvey, were part of a gang called the Trent Tigers, and the six were suspected of grassing on them.'

'Those are things beyond my control, I'm afraid. The current DCS in Castlewood is in favour of it but cannot commit to it as yet,' Denison said. 'There would be an outcry if it became public knowledge. You know what the press and online media are like.'

'Hmm, I suppose.' Harrison looked thoughtful. 'There are too many friends of my supposed former colleagues in here. I would need to move to somewhere safer to start with. That is non-negotiable.'

'If these "former colleagues" were arrested and you suddenly were relocated, it would be like a big arrow pointing at you. Inevitable conclusions would be jumped to,' said Denison.

'Hmm, that is a problem but I would not last a week in here, Mr Denison.' He was visibly shaking. His face had gone pale. Paler even than the normal prison paleness.

'That I can understand. I shall ask the governor about it before I leave. So, are you prepared to give me a few names? Or, at least, state as a fact that Malone and his pal colluded in this latest killing?' Denison was on tenterhooks. Everything rested on Harrison's reply.

'I could say that, if you lot would first promise to seek a parole hearing, and I am moved. A move is mandatory. Without parole, I am facing another twenty years, at least.'

'I shall need to chat to the DCS and see what can be done,' said Denison. He was not hopeful. He decided to leave it at that. No point in making rash promises.

Chapter 13
Harrison Has Conditions

As I expected, Denison appeared in my office again. He did not look happy.

'Good morning, Walter,' I said cheerfully. 'Have you any news?'

'Well, sort of,' he replied. 'Harrison all but admitted he had accomplices and that Malone and Harvey were behind the recent killing of Fred Mulgrew. They were behind the six killings albeit from prison. Seems they murdered the original Mulgrew, Wally, by mistake and only found out a few months ago. So, they had Fred done too. They, Malone and Harvey, were part of a gang called the Trent Tigers, and the six were grassing on them.' He was reading notes he had made when he left Harrison.

'That's a good start,' I said.

'But he has conditions. He wants a move to a safer prison pending a parole board hearing. Of course, he also wants a new identity when released. If he is released.'

'I suppose those are only to be expected in the circumstances.' I paused and thought for a few moments. Walter was silent. Eventually, I said, 'The only thing I can think of is I will put it to a bigwig at the Home Office, naming no names, to get his opinion. The government will not want a public backlash if its "tough on crime" policy is undermined. If it is a non-starter, we shall just have to drop the whole idea. Sorry, but that is the bottom line.' I could see the disappointment on Denison's face.

'I understand,' he replied. 'Okay, try that, Jacob. I'll then let Harrison know the result.' Denison stood and shook hands. He left, looking desolate. There was nothing else I could do. And I was not hopeful.

As promised, I phoned my Home Office contact on a secure line. I could not take the chance on a leak.

'Good morning, Sir Geoffrey,' I said. 'Jacob Marley here. Thank you for taking my call.'

'No problem, Jacob. Been a long time since we spoke. Do you recall the good old days at Clarendon Public School? We got into some scrapes then, old bean.' He chuckled.

'Yes, we certainly did,' I replied, with a laugh. 'I recall the prank we played on old "Toffee" Appleby, the chemistry master.' They both laughed. 'We must get together soon for a catch-up.'

'Yes, certainly. I'll get my secretary to contact you. Up to the eyes here at the moment. The prime minister is phoning every ten minutes with a new problem, what? So, what can I do for you?'

'It is a rather tricky situation, Geoffrey. We have a convicted chap serving life, who is willing to name names for a recent killing and the murders twenty years ago of six informers. You may recall them?' I said.

'Oh yes. Ghastly business, as I recall. Absolutely ghastly. I suppose this chap wants certain concessions for his information?' Sir Geoffrey said.

'Well, it is only to be expected,' I replied. 'He wants an immediate move to a safer prison pending a parole board, plus a new identity if he is released.'

'Hmm, not asking much, is he? Still, it is logical, I suppose. He will be in danger if his fellow inmates find out. I wondered why you wanted a secure line.

'Of course, I cannot just promise all this off the top of my head, Jacob. The P.M. would have to be consulted. Do you think this chap's information would be worth the storm of criticism that would result?'

I cleared my throat. 'Well, it could result in several killers being put away. Two, at least, for the recent murder, and an unknown number, at least four, for the six historic killings,' I replied.

I could almost hear Geoffrey's brain whirring. Counting possible votes.

After a few moments, he continued, 'Personally speaking, I think it is worth a try, but, and it is a big but, I shall have to consult the boss, Jacob. I'll be in touch. Bye for now.' He hung up.

I sat holding the receiver for several seconds in a sort of trance. Had he really agreed to the idea in principle? I almost shouted with glee but refrained just in time.

I asked my secretary to get Walter on the line.

'Walter, Jacob here. I've some good news for you,' I said.

'Oh, good. I could do with some just now, our cat just died. Had him for years. The missus is in tears,' Denison replied.

'Oh, sorry to hear that, but I have had a chat with that friend in the H.O. and he is going to consult the boss; you know whom I mean,' I said.

'Ah yes, I can guess who. Do you think he will go for it?' Denison asked.

'Tricky, to say the least. If the media get hold of the story, it could have serious consequences. I'll let you know in due course. Bye for now. Busy, busy, busy.' I rang off. I knew Walter would continue to ask questions if I did not stop him.

Denison said to Millicent, 'That was Jacob. He is hopeful of getting movement on the Harrison thing.

'Shall we bury the cat in the garden? Under the cherry tree would be a nice spot,' he said softly, changing the subject.

His wife replied, 'That would be a nice spot, yes. Shall we do it now, before it rains?'

'I'll just dig a hole. Bring him out in a few minutes.'

Denison grabbed the little-used rusty garden spade and dug a hole about two feet deep. Millicent brought Cedric IV out, wrapped in a towel, and placed him in the hole. Denison filled it in and patted the earth down with the spade. They stood silently for a few minutes.

'I'll plant some bulbs in a day or two. Crocuses, purple ones I think. They'll look nice there. Let's have a cup of tea, Dear,' he said and they went indoors.

Half an hour later, the doorbell rang. They both jumped at the sudden noise. Dennison went slowly to the door. His wife was still too upset.

'Dennison? Delivery for you, guv,' said a man in a tan-coloured work coat.

'We aren't expecting a parcel,' Denison said looking puzzled. The man held a large cardboard box with several holes in the side.

'From Barclay's Pet Store, guv. Man named Marley called in and paid for it to be delivered.' The man handed over the box. He then went back to his van.

Denison set the box down on the hall table and opened it. 'Millicent, come and see! You'll never believe it!' He sounded excited.

Millicent hurried out of the kitchen. 'What's all the fuss ab…? Oh, goodness,' she put her hands to the cheeks. 'I don't believe it. A kitten! A lovely kitten and so like our dear Cedric!'

'Jacob sent him. We shall call him Cedric.' Denison stopped and checked. 'No, it's a little girl. I don't know if there is a feminine of Cedric. Shall we call her Cedrica?'

'Oh yes, what else could we call her?' Millicent agreed. 'Phone Jacob and thank him.'

Cedrica miaowed, *I need food, slave!* She seemed to know she had landed a cushy number. *More humans I can twist around my little finger…if I had a little finger.*

Chapter 14
His Majesty's Opposition Is
Quite Keen on Finding Fault

'Good morning, Sir Geoffrey, you sounded rather agitated when you telephoned,' said the prime minister. He stood and reached across his desk to shake hands. 'Do sit down.'

'Good morning, Prime Minister. Yes, I was rather. I have received some welcome news. It may, hopefully, help our standing as regards Law and Order. The Party's stance has received a deal of criticism of late,' Sir Geoffrey replied.

'Hmm, I do hope so. His Majesty's Opposition is quite keen on finding fault,' the P.M. replied.

Sir Geoffrey said, 'I'll be as succinct as possible, Prime Minister. You may recall some twenty years ago the dreadful slaughter of six men in Staffordshire. The prime minister nodded. Well, it appears the fellow, who was found guilty, has indicated that he would name his accomplices in exchange for a possible parole release and a change of identity.'

'Hmm, would he indeed? How many were involved? And how many years has he served?' the prime minister asked.

'He has not actually said how many, Prime Minister, but there must have been several. One man could not have captured six individuals on his own. He has been incarcerated for some twenty years, I believe.'

The prime minister replied, 'Twenty years! Of a life term, is it? What might the voters think if he were released, I wonder? One needs to be very careful in these cases. You know what the press is like.'

'Yes, it was life and no doubt there will be an outcry, but the other culprits are still free, Prime Minister. A danger to the public we could stress. Who knows what crimes they may have committed since? Moreover, the lifer is prepared to implicate two other fellows in a more recent murder. I cannot recall the names, but a local detective superintendent is keen to catch them,' Sir Geoffrey said.

'Hmm, yes,' the prime minister steepled his fingers and thought for a minute. He was always careful about decisions of this type. Public opinion can be fickle as any politician knows. 'Yes, we can stress the benefits of locking up several criminals as against releasing one on parole. If he gives several names and they are convicted, of course, a new identity will be no problem, I am sure. It has been done before. Proceed with care, Sir Geoffrey. Keep me informed.

'Now, I must dash. Cabinet meeting in ten minutes—the climate protestors are causing bother again. One had hoped that they would have, er, melted away by now.' He chuckled.

'Yes, I shall tread carefully, and thank you, Prime Minister.' Sir Geoffrey left quickly.

After he reached his office, he telephoned me.

'Hello, Jacob, good news. The prime minister is, shall we say, broadly in favour of trying to get parole for that chap, provided he gives the names and they are convicted. It's up to the parole board of course. One cannot be seen to interfere with their decisions.'

'Well, thank you, Geoffrey. That is good news indeed,' I replied.

'Of course, we need to be careful. The voters would not like a multiple murderer released without some very good benefit from it. That is, a good number of villains locked up,' said Sir Geoffrey.

'Yes, very understandable. We will have to try to keep the voters happy. The problem all politicians have, I'm afraid,' I said. 'Politics and principles do not always mix well.'

I passed this news on to Denison. He was, shall we say, overjoyed. I could almost imagine him jumping for joy as he spoke on the phone.

'That is tremendous news,' Denison said. 'I shall arrange a visit with him straight away. I am pleased the offer of a new identity is thought essential, and it is good to be able to tell him it is not a problem. I will get back to you as soon as I have spoken with him—Oh, many thanks for the kitten. It was most kind of you. Cedrica we have named her. The wife is thrilled. Bye, Jacob.' Denison was gleeful.

Denison telephoned the prison governor immediately and at ten o'clock the next day, he arrived at the prison. He took a seat in the interview room and awaited Harrison.

Presently, a senior prison officer entered and looking rather sheepish, said, 'Mr Denison, I'm afraid I have some rather distressing news.' Denison went pale in anticipation.

The officer continued, 'The prisoner, Harrison, has just been found dead in his cell. He appears to have been murdered. Well, has obviously been murdered.'

'Murdered! In his cell! How is that possible?' Denison was almost speechless. 'I mean, who would have access to it?'

'Sorry, that we do not know as yet. There is little doubt it was murder. His throat was cut, blood everywhere: on the floor, walls, everything is soaked in it. He put up a struggle obviously. We will be checking the cameras, the CCTV, so hopefully, we can see who did it. In the meantime, that is all I can tell you, Mr Denison.'

'Yes, thank you, Officer. Will you ask the governor to let me know the outcome, please?' Denison said, his voice almost gone. *Talk about one disappointment after another,* he thought.

'Of course. Let me show you out,' said the officer.

Back at home, Denison told his wife the news.

'Oh, how horrible. That poor man. I know he was a convicted killer, but I can't help feeling sorry for him,' Millicent replied. 'Murdered in his cell! How absolutely dreadful.'

'Yes, I know. It was a terrible end. He must have put up a fight as there was a lot of blood everywhere, according to the officer.

'It is also the end of the search for his gang. He was the only one who knew the names as far as we know. It is so frustrating. I was this close to getting the names.' He held a finger and thumb about an inch apart as an illustration. Denison thumped a table in anger. His wife was startled and the new cat fled into the kitchen.

'Don't be upset, Dear. You have done all you could. Just try to forget it. Something may turn up and Jacob Marley can deal with it,' his wife said.

'Yes, you are right. I've done what I could.' He sighed. 'I think I shall mow the lawn.' He stood and went out with a heavy heart.

Mrs Denison thought, *Things must be bad if he is mowing the lawn without me nagging him.*

Chapter 15
The Missing-Finger-Guy Must Be Somewhere

When I heard the news about Colin Harrison, I was beyond disappointed. I was certain we would soon be making arrests. Denison had phoned me. He sounded so depressed I was quite concerned about him. I tried to help by assuring him that if anything new occurred I would let him know. I would still be pursuing the search for the missing-finger-guy. He must be somewhere.

I spoke to my officers, 'You have all heard about Harrison, I'm sure?' They all nodded.

DS Daniel Parker said, 'Yes, boss, it's all over the newspapers. They are saying there's nowhere safe from knife crime. But at least, in this case, there is a limited number of suspects.'

'This is a setback, but the case is still open, as is the case of the murder of Fred Mulgrew.'

James Kavenagh said, 'If we find the killer, it could lead to the rest of the gang which did the six informers back in the day, sir. The name Mulgrew featured in both. It's hardly a common name in these parts.'

'Quite right,' I said. 'Let's keep the pressure on the local wrong-uns and something will turn up. I feel it in my bones.' They all laughed at my little jest. It always pays to humour the boss!

Mrs Denison exclaimed after three days of her husband moping around the house—he was still half-heartedly doing chores around the place, 'Walter, if you cannot forget about Malone and what's his name, go back to Marley and see if there is anything with which you can help. Trawling CCTV or something…anything. You are driving me up the walls.' Denison was really getting on her nerves.

Denison perked up. 'Thank you, Dear, I think I shall do that. My heart is not in papering walls and stuff. I just need to be doing something. I wonder how most people can just switch tracks when they leave work. Policing is in my blood. My ancestors must have been Tudor law enforcers or whatever they had.' They both laughed. His wife tried to picture Denison in the Tudor breeches that looked like pumpkins and woollen stockings. *No no, most definitely no,* she thought.

'I'll pay a visit to Jacob in a day or two. I think I shall look up a few old snitches down the pub near where Malone is staying. There may be some rumours I could get a hint from as to what he is up to.'

A few days later in my office.

'Good morning, Jacob,' Denison said as he entered. 'How are you? Well, I hope.'

'Morning, Walter,' I replied. 'Yes, I am fine, thank you.' Truth be told, I was beginning to find his visits a bit annoying.

96

'Terrible news about your prisoner chap. I have just this minute received an email from the prison governor,' I continued.

'Oh! Anything interesting?' Denison asked.

'Well, they found the culprit. A prisoner who is probably a relative of Malone's; he goes by the name of Alex Malone, overheard an officer speaking of you meeting Harrison. He put two and two together and decided he, Harrison, was about to spill the beans on the six killings and the more recent murder. We are checking for a family connection.'

Denison was agog. 'So, there is a link possibly connecting Sidney Malone to all the murders. Just as I suspected.'

I continued, 'Yes, when the body was found, there was an immediate search of all the cells. This Malone fella was in his cell a few metres away trying to wash the blood off his clothing, and himself. He was saturated in it. He was wrapped in a towel and taken straight to a secure cell in the isolation wing. It is an open-and-shut case. But we are checking the blood DNA just to be certain. He'll be behind bars for the rest of his life.'

'So, if we, er, you can prove he is a relative of Sid Malone, you can lean on him to implicate Sid. This is the best news I have heard since…since the last time I had good news.' Denison chuckled.

'You can rely on me, Walter. I shall lean on him big-time.' I then told him I had another appointment and would be in touch. Denison was walking on air.

'Millicent, Jacob has a lead on Sidney Malone. The killer in the prison is a relative of his no less. At least, there is a good chance he is. Jacob is going to squeeze a

97

confession from him that implicates Sid in the death of Mulgrew and the six informers.' Denison was jubilant.

'Oh, that's good, Dear,' his wife replied. *Maybe we will have peace at last,* she thought.

Denison put on a pair of slippers, sat in his favourite chair and put his feet up.

Cedrica arose slowly from the rug in front of the fire. She had claimed possession of it like her predecessor. She stretched and tried to jump on Denison's lap. Being a tiny kitten she could not manage the height. Tiny claws dug into Denison's leg.

'Ouch!' he cried. 'You little beast.'

'She's only a kitten, Walter. Lift her up,' his wife said. Denison lifted the kitten onto his lap.

Denison was stunned. This was the first time the cat had shown any interest in being petted. Denison stroked Cedrica and was rewarded with loud purring.

'Oh, Cedrica has taken a shine to you, Walter. That's nice,' his wife said. 'Now relax. Have a pipe, as long as you open the window. Tea?'

'A nice cuppa would be most welcome, Dearest. Most welcome indeed.' Soon, clouds of pipe smoke were exiting via the window. Things were definitely brighter: permission to smoke his pipe! Wonders never cease.

His wife set the tray of teapot and cups and assorted biscuits on a table. Denison was fond of chocolate ones.

'Yes, it seems we are now best buddies, Cedrica and I,' Denison said. He helped himself to a chocolate digestive and then tapped his pipe out in an ashtray. Even he found two hands inadequate to eat, drink and smoke at the same time. Eating was always to be preferred even to his pipe.

That night, he slept soundly secure in the knowledge that Malone and Harvey would soon be back behind bars.

Chapter 16
If Only We Could Trace the Three-Fingered-Bloke

At our next meeting, I said to Denison, 'There is still no way of connecting Malone to the murders. Alex Malone is not talking.'

Denison replied, 'I felt that this relative was unlikely to be forthcoming with evidence, but I am confident we will find something, Jacob. If only we could trace the three-fingered-bloke.'

Sid Malone and Harvey, meanwhile, were more than happy to hear that Colin Harrison had been eliminated. They were at Harvey's residence.

'That bloke could have sunk us both, mate,' Sid said to Harvey.

'Yeah, he would have named all the others who did them informers back in the day,' Harvey replied. 'And they would have named us. Harrison also could have guessed arranged for that Fred Mulgrew to be done a while ago. We got the wrong brother back in the day. It was Fred we wanted.'

Malone said, 'Yes, Fred Mulgrew found out, somehow, that we had got Harrison's gang to do in his brother, Wally Mulgrew. Fred was thinking of going to the cops. Too many loose tongues in this town if you ask me.'

'Perhaps we should cut out a few tongues!' Harvey said, and both laughed.

'Anyway, changing the subject,' Malone said, 'what about that job we were going to pull? Let's forget the post office and rob a bank like in the good old days.'

'Yeah, for sure. Love doing a bank, I do. What about that old bank in Burton we did before?' Harvey suggested.

Malone replied, 'Nah, was in it a couple of weeks ago, just out of curiosity. They have all kinds of security there now. You would need a Centurian tank to get in now: like Fort Knox in that Bond movie it is, minus the U S army.'

'No matter. Plenty more around. What about Lichfield? There's the South Staffordshire Savings Bank. It is pretty old. We could give it a once over. What do you think?' Harvey said.

'Yes, okay. That could be worth a try,' replied Malone. 'Let's borrow a motor tomorrow and drive over there, mate. Have you any false registration plates left?'

'Yeah, I do as it happens. They are those stick-on plastic ones. You just peel off the backing and stick them on the existing plates. I know a bloke who makes them. Easy peasy.'

'Excellent. Sticky-backed plastic like used to be on Blue Peter on TV.'

'Well, I'm off home. Can't keep me eyes open. I'll give you a call in the morning,' Malone said. They had obtained new pay-as-you-go mobile phones unknown to the police.

'Right, see you in the morning.' Harvey yawned loudly as he closed the door.

Next morning, Harvey entered the Malone home via the back garden. He was taking no chances of being followed. They had not seen any cops in weeks—even Denison had not appeared.

'Morning, Jake,' said George Malone, cheerfully. 'What are you guys planning? Sid is full of beans this morning.'

'Planning a job, aren't we? You interested in lending a hand?' said Harvey.

'Yeah, sure. No problem. Just don't tell the missus. She'd go ballistic if she knew.' George grimaced.

Harvey laughed. 'Okay, Mum's the word. My cousin, Tom, has pulled out. His girlfriend actually did go ballistic when she found out what he was planning. She started chucking things about. He has a lump on the side of his head.'

'Where's Sid?' Harvey continued.

'Having a shower. Said he thinks better after a wash. Oh, that's him trying to sing.' A series of noises could be heard from upstairs which vaguely resembled singing.

♪*Oh, what a beautiful morning, oh, what a beautiful day. I've got a beautiful feeling, I'll rob a bank toooo-daaaaay!*♪

George grimaced. 'So much for secrecy. The missus will hear him.'

Then came a shout from the master bedroom, 'George Malone, if you think you are going robbing, think again!' Daisy was removing her hair curlers, a daily ritual.

'Never crossed my mind, Dearest,' George shouted. He grimaced again.

'You had better not, or else,' Daisy replied. She was not a person to beat around the bush.

When Sid Malone came downstairs, George was furious. 'What do you mean by letting Daisy know about the bank job, Sid? Of all the stupid stunts. Now I'll never hear the end of it. I have a good mind to pull out of the whole business.'

'Oh, sorry, Geordie. I wasn't thinking. I'll tell her I was only messing about,' Malone said, looking guilty.

'You had better,' George replied. 'Now, we need to go out somewhere to discuss our plan. We are off to the park, Daisy,' he shouted.

The three of them went to a nearby park looking like the characters in "Last of the Summer Wine" on television. Sitting on a bench Sid Malone said, 'Right, we will have a look around that bank in Lichfield to see the setup. Provided the security is not too tight we can hit it this weekend.'

They selected a car in the carpark—a nice little Ford. Nothing too noticeable. Nobody was in sight so Harvey stuck the fake registration plates on and they drove off.

Fifteen minutes later, they arrived in Lichfield and parked near the target. They wandered past the bank casually, pretending to be window shopping.

Sid Malone said, 'Right, I'll go in and have a look around. After a minute or two, I'll pretend to have forgotten my wallet and leave. You guys wait in that café across the street. Okay?'

Malone entered the bank and had a quick glance, with a practised eye, to spot cameras. Then he went to a table where there were withdrawal and lodgement slips. He selected one and then began to search his pockets as if he had forgotten his wallet. His eyes were roaming the room picking out security points. A large oak door, set in a rear wall, was open. Malone could see the large safe. A security man stood near the exit. Sid made a show of giving up his search and made for the exit. The security man stepped in front of him. 'Excuse me, sir, I cannot help noticing you were having a problem. May I assist?'

Taken by surprise, Malone mumbled, 'Oh, ah, no it's okay, mate. Just forgot my wallet, didn't I? I would forget my head if it weren't screwed on.'

The man laughed. 'Oh, okay, sir. Have a good day.' The man stepped aside, touching the brim of his hat by way of a salute.

Once outside, Malone breathed a sigh of relief. He walked to the café and sat down with the other two in Benny's Eatery.

'Had a narrow squeak, guys,' he said. 'Was stopped by a helpful security guard! I was sure he had sussed what I was doing. Saw the safe though.'

'Hmm, what is the safe like? What make is it?' asked George Malone, an experienced safecracker.

Sid replied, 'From what I could see, it is a Gaston and Webb Ultra about ten, maybe twenty years old.'

'Hmm, interesting. I have done one of those before, in Manchester. Shouldn't be a problem.'

Harvey said, 'Okay, let's wander round to the back of the building and see what's what.'

'Best go one at a time so as not to attract unwanted attention,' Sid Malone suggested.

Ten minutes later, the three of them met in an alley at the back gate to the bank. They stood for minutes noting the lock on the gate and the cameras—six in all.

'It's not going to be easy getting past that lot,' Harvey remarked.

'Oi! What's your game? What're yous lot up to?' A loud voice made them start. 'What're yous lot hangin' aroun' here for? Clear off!' It was a security guard, with a distinct Ulster accent, all six and a half feet of him, who had been having a crafty snooze behind some bins.

Malone was the first to recover. 'Oh, er, we are looking for our dog, mate. Have you seen him by any chance? Black and white mongrel, about so high.' He indicated the height from the ground.

Harvey played along and shouted, 'Rover, here boy!' He whistled.

'No, I've seen no dog. Clear off, the lot of yous afore I call the cops.'

'Okay, okay, keep your hair on,' said George Malone. 'No need to get shirty, mate.' Then he noticed the man was as bald as a billiard ball.

'Are you takin' the Michael? Be off with yah. I'll not be tellin' yous again,' the man shouted, his face red with anger.

The three friends murmured apologies and made a hasty retreat back to the street. They shouted the dog's name for effect.

Back at the Malone residence, they sat and laughed. 'That was a laugh,' said Sid. 'You saying about him keeping his hair on…'

'…and him bald as a coot,' Harvey finished the sentence. George laughed.

Sid Malone looked serious and said, 'We can forget about going in the back way. They probably have a guard on day and night.'

'Yeah, and all those cameras,' said Harvey. 'It will be difficult if not impossible to get in the front though, as it is on a main street.'

'What about we get some shooters and just walk in?' George suggested.

'Oh, no way. I have never been one for guns and stuff,' said Sid. He shook his head.

'Me neither,' said Harvey.

'We don't need to actually fire them. Just wave them around, and shout a lot,' George said. 'Marvellous what a bit of shouting will do!'

'I suppose we could get blanks. Make a lot of noise, they would,' Sid said.

'That sounds good. As long as no one actually gets hurt. Judges take a dim view of people getting shot,' Harvey said. 'But how will we get them guns? I don't know anyone.'

George said, 'I can get a couple off A P, an old pal. He might even join us if you guys don't mind a smaller split.'

'A P?' Sid queried.

'Oh, it's short for "Accident Prone". Real name Dave Smith. He's always tripping or falling or something. Lost a little finger about six months ago when working on a homemade pistol. He was using a cutter to make the barrel when he accidentally chopped the finger off.'

'Ouch! Sounds painful.' Harvey asked, 'Could he not get it sewn back on?'

'Nah, he could hardly say he was making a gun and he had an accident,' said George, laughing.

The other two laughed. 'I suppose not,' said Harvey.

George said, 'He told me he was the driver of the getaway car when you had that Fred Mulgrew shot.'

'Really?' Sid gasped. 'He is the bloke the cops are searching for! Wow! Our man must have hired him as a driver.'

'We owe him a vote of thanks,' said Harvey.

George continued, 'I'll tell you a funny story 'bout him. He and a mate were holding up a bank some ten years ago. The bank manager was old school and wasn't taking any nonsense, as he called it. "What do you chaps mean by coming in here frightening my customers? Be off with you", he shouted. The two lads were so surprised they froze. The manager was a big bloke grabbed Accident Prone by the coat collar and frog-marched him to the door. The mate scarpered sharpish. Two security guards grabbed A P. They pinned him against a wall. Just then a protest march came by, lots of shouting and chanting slogans: Ban the Bomb or Save the Whale, or something. A cop was walking beside them to keep them moving. The manager shouted for the cop to arrest Accident Prone but the cop just ignored him and walked on. The manager was furious and ran after the cop. The two security guards kind of took their attention off their prisoner and A P legged it as fast as his pins would carry him.' The others laughed.

'Okay, that's what we will do: get some shooters with blanks. How about Friday, if I can get the shooters?' George said.

And so it was agreed that on the Friday, Harvey would be the driver while the two Malones, Sid and George, and Dave Smith, if willing, entered the bank. That was the plan.

Would it succeed? Or would Accident Prone live up to his nickname?

At ten o'clock on Friday morning, Harvey had to drive past the bank three times before there was a place to stop. They all pulled on masks and Sid, Dave and George went inside shouting and waving their guns.

Sid went up to the counter past the queue and shouted, 'This is a robbery. Open the safe and hand over the cash!'

However, he had not reckoned on the formidable Miss Alicia Jackson—think Boadicea, Emmeline Pankhurst and Margaret Thatcher rolled into one—the assistant manager who was acting as a teller. The usual person had called in sick much to Miss Jackson's annoyance. 'Can't you see there is a queue, young man? Please await your turn,' she commanded, looking over her glasses. The other customers were amazed and stood open-mouthed waiting to see what would happen.

George and Dave, meanwhile, had the security guard standing with his arms in the air. Sid felt as useless as a water pistol fighting a bonfire. What to do?

'Look, lady, this is a stick-up, a robbery and if you don't want to be shot—' Sid began.

'I have told you once, young man, await your turn. I dislike having to repeat myself,' retorted Miss Jackson. 'Now, Mr Andrews, you wish to make a lodgement?' she said to a very bemused customer.

'Er, yes,' said Mr Andrews who was first in the queue. He proffered his savings book and twenty pounds.

Sid was confused and hesitated. George fired a shot in the air. 'Lady, get the safe opened or this here guard gets shot dead.' The guard gulped. There was a hole in the ceiling. *They are supposed to be only blanks!* thought Sid.

Dave shouted, 'Open the safe…NOW!' *Butch Cassidy and Sundance never had this bother,* he thought. He was a Robert Redford fan.

'Oh, very well,' said Miss Jackson, grumpily, and she made her way to the safe.

Just then, the guard out in the backyard burst through the rear door. 'What's going on? I heard a shot.' He stopped mid-stride and raised his hands when he saw Sid's gun pointing at him.

Sid was actually more scared than the guard. Things were definitely not going to plan. Miss Jackson was fiddling with the combination lock, her hands shaking, and she eventually got the door open.

'There you are, one empty safe,' she said with a smirk. She stood back looking triumphant.

Sid looked into the safe and saw empty shelves, except for a few hundred pounds in used five-pound notes. 'Where's all the cash?' he demanded. 'I've heard of a pub with no beer…but a bank with no cash!'

'There isn't any,' said Miss Jackson firmly. 'The security firm is on strike and we have received nothing all week.' She suppressed a smirk as she neglected to say that the week's takings were in another safe in another room.

Sid looked at George who shouted, 'Grab what's there and let's get out of here.'

Sid grabbed the fivers and stuffed them into a bag. The three dashed out to the car. Harvey sped off just as a police car appeared around a corner. Several other cars had braked heavily and blocked the street, accidentally enabling the getaway.

'Get down a side street and ditch the car. Split up and meet back at mine,' George ordered. Harvey drove about half a mile and stopped. The four of them ran off in different directions. They headed back to George's home eventually.

'And just where have you four been, may I ask?' said Daisy Malone. scowling with arms folded.

'Er, nowhere, Dear,' George mumbled. 'Just out for a walk in the park.' He looked decidedly guilty.

'A likely story. I have just been listening to the news on the radio. It seems three idiots tried to rob a bank in Lichfield, and a fourth was in a getaway car. Tried to rob a bank with no money. Who in their right mind robs a bank when there is a security delivery strike? Who? Four complete idiots, that's who. No one is sending lodgements to the banks.'

'Er, what made you think it was us?' asked Sid Malone defensively.

'Because I am looking at the four idiots in question,' Daisy replied. There was a lot of foot-shuffling.

'Okay, it was us, but we wore masks, didn't we? The cops will never find us,' George replied.

A loud knock came to the front door. They all nearly jumped out of their skins.

'Who can that be?' asked Harvey stupidly.

'The cops, probably,' answered Daisy, glaring at him.

'Couldn't be. We was very careful,' said Sid.

'Yeah, we never left no clues,' said George. 'Go and answer it, Daisy.'

Daisy glared at the four, then went to the door.

'Good afternoon, Madam. May I have a word?' a bloke at the door said. 'I'm from the gas company…' Daisy and the four idiots breathed a sigh of relief. 'There have been complaints about the smell of gas in the area. Have you had any untoward nasty smells at all?'

'Only my husband's feet,' replied Daisy. 'Now, if that is all? Goodbye.' She shut the door before the man could say more. He stood for several seconds open-mouthed.

'What did you have to say that for, about my feet? They don't pong; not much anyway,' George said.

'It was the first thing that entered my head. Now, do you see what you have done? I'm a bundle of nerves, thanks to you lot.' Her hands were shaking. 'And it said there was a shot fired. A shot? Where did you get guns, may I ask?'

'Sorry, Daisy,' said Sid. 'It won't happen again.' He glared at George who looked embarrassed.

Harvey quickly said, 'I'm off home before anything else happens. Sorry, Mrs Malone, but the guns were not supposed to be loaded. If I had known, I would never have been involved.' He looked pointedly at George and then slipped out through the back door and headed home.

Dave Smith mumbled something and left too.

Daisy stayed silent for a few moments which seemed like hours for the Malones. 'If that Dave "Accident Prone" fella enters this house again, I am leaving. Understood?'

Yes, Dear,' said George.

'Yes, Daisy,' said Sid.

'He's bad luck, he is,' said Daisy. Dave's ears must have been burning.

The Chief Constable of the region had asked Detectives Sanderson, Parker and me to assist the Lichfield police in identifying the would-be bank robbers. Witnesses had said they had a local accent, possibly the Burton upon Trent area.

CCTV recording was played over a few times. We listened carefully to the voices of the two men. Their masks tended to muffle the speech but they were definitely from eastern Staffordshire.

DS Daniel Parker said finally, 'Those two sort of look familiar, the part of the faces we can see. And the voice of the one near the safe. I just cannot place it.'

'Same here,' said DS Robin Sanderson. 'Let me think about it for a while. It will come back to me'

I said, 'I am only new in the area, sir, so the voices mean nothing to me.' I hesitated and then suggested to the Chief Constable, 'Do you know, sir, there is one man who might know them?'

'Who might that be?' he asked.

'Walter Denison, sir. He will know nearly every criminal in the county,' I replied.

'Hmm, he is retired, isn't he?' the Chief asked. I nodded. 'Well, send a car for him, pronto.' A car was sent immediately to Denison's address. Meanwhile, we all had a cup of coffee, while we waited.

Denison threw on a coat as soon as the driver called at his door. Mrs Denison was not pleased. She thought, *Don't blame me if your dinner is in the cat!*

'I'll be back soon, Dear,' he shouted over his shoulder as he hurried to the car. On the way to the police station, the driver filled him in on the events of the morning. Denison had heard of the robbery on the radio and was beyond excited.

'Hmm, I wonder,' Denison had muttered to himself. 'Could it be Malone and Harvey? Sounds like the sort of stunt they would try…but armed robbery? Not their usual activity. They favour knives and they are more the breaking and entering type.'

I said, when Denison arrived in the Lichfield police HQ, 'Ah, Walter old chap, we have some interesting CCTV from the bank job. Did my driver fill you in?'

'Less of the old,' Denison chuckled. 'I'm hoping it is our old adversaries Malone and Harvey.'

'Difficult to tell. They are masked and armed. Malone is more of a knife carrier. Still, have a look will you?'

'Alright, start the machine.' The CCTV started a few minutes before the three robbers entered.

'This is them coming in now,' I said, unnecessarily as the robbers entered.

After a few seconds, it reached the point where the guard was standing at gunpoint. Denison said, 'I don't recognise that bloke,' indicating Dave Smith. 'He could be a relative or friend of Malone's. Now, the one at the safe, I would know those shifty eyes anywhere. That is Sid Malone, I'm pretty sure. I'd wager my pension on it. I have interviewed that bloke more times than I could count. I wonder where Harvey was?'

I replied, 'There was a getaway driver. So there were four of them altogether. We found the car abandoned a half mile away. It had been stolen that morning. No prints or anything, of course, and we would need more proof than a similarity of eyes, I'm afraid. Crown Prosecution Service would never accept it.'

'Okay,' Denison said. 'It would be worth lifting the three of them and that other man, whoever he is, for questioning. If we can get his name. What d'you think, Jacob?'

'Certainly worth a try.' I spoke to an officer standing nearby. 'Sergeant Baird, get a couple of cars to their addresses. Pick up the two Malones and Harvey and the other bloke if he's about.'

'Yes, sir,' Sergeant Artie Baird replied, with a grin. 'Be a pleasure.' He shouted at a number of constables. 'You, you and you, follow me.' They piled into cars and drove off.

Chapter 17
Stay Cool

George Malone, at a front bay window, shouted to Sid, 'Hey, two cop cars just stopped outside. The fuzz must be on to us.'

'How can they be? We wore masks, we did. They can only be fishing. Stay cool.' Sid made hand gestures to indicate "staying cool".

'Alright for you, but I don't want another spell inside. We did an armed robbery. Do you know how many years that will be?' George replied.

'What's all the fuss about?' asked Daisy entering from the kitchen, wiping her hands on a towel.

'The fuzz, the cops, are here. Look out of the window,' said George.

'Oh, good heavens, I knew this would end badly. You'll be locked up again, and do not expect me to be waiting for you coming out.' Daisy was furious. 'I won't be a jail-widow again.'

'It's just the cops looking for someone to blame,' said Sid. 'They cannot have any proof. They are only chancing their arm.' There was a loud rap on the door. The three looked at each other. 'Don't forget the alibi we have agreed.'

'Well! Go and answer it, George,' Daisy said loudly.

George went into the hall and opened the front door. He cleared his throat and said, 'Yes, officer, how…how can I help you?'

'We need you to come to the station. You and Sidney Malone,' Sergeant Baird replied.

George was speechless until Sid appeared at his side. 'What's this about, officer? We haven't done nothing.'

'That's a double negative, Mr Malone. Means you have done something. Now, get into the car, there's a good chap. Let's not have any fuss,' said the sergeant. He had his hand on the handcuffs on his belt.

Sid, whose knowledge of English grammar was almost non-existent, was lost for words, so he and George walked to the police car.

Another car, meanwhile, had picked up Harvey. Thomas Paton was not at home. He had gone on holiday.

'Well, well, Sidney Malone, as I live and breathe, we meet once more,' said Denison. 'Been up to your old tricks again, eh? Plus armed robbery this time?' He sat at a table in an interview room.

'I, er, I don't know what you mean, Mr Denison. And aren't you retired? This cannot be legal.' Sid looked smug.

'It certainly is as DCS Marley is present. I'm sure you have heard of him!' said Denison.

Sid shook his head and said, 'I want a solicitor. You lot cannot just lift people from their homes without cause. We have rights. *Magna Carta* and all that stuff.'

Denison pushed a photograph of the bank robber across the table. 'Recognise anyone, Malone?'

Sid lifted the photo and glanced at it. 'Nope, I've no idea. It is just some bloke in a mask is all. Could be anyone.' He smirked. 'Could be the President of France, for all I know. Looks a bit like Tom Cruise actually.'

'Look at his eyes,' said Denison. 'Shifty, beady eyes just like yours. And the big thick eyebrows.' He folded his arms and sat back.

Sid Malone looked again. 'Nah, nothing like my peepers, Mr Denison. Must be thousands of guys with thick eyebrows. You've got the wrong man.' He sniggered. 'You must be getting too old for this police work.' He emphasised too old.

I interrupted, 'That's not what George Malone said. You got the shooters. He is confessing all as we speak.' Denison nodded in agreement.

'He's the one...' Sid realised he had fallen for the trap. 'I'm saying nothing.' *He's only bluffing,* he thought.

Meanwhile, in another room, George Malone was also being interviewed by DI Harry Trevelyan and DI James Kavenagh.

'Now, Mr Malone, may I call you George, so as not to confuse the recording with your relative?' Harry asked.

'Knock yourself out, Detective,' George shrugged. He sat back, looking smug.

Harry suppressed a grin. 'A bank robbery, or should I say, an attempted bank robbery, took place earlier today. A CCTV photo of one person firing a weapon closely resembles someone in this room, namely, you.' He passed a photo across the table.

George picked it up and glanced at it. 'You cannot see his face, assuming it is a male. How can you possibly say that is me?' He laughed.

'The shifty eyes for one thing. Also, the clothes you were wearing, are at this moment being examined for gunshot residue. Plus your hands and hair were swabbed when you arrived. You may have washed your hands but it is unlikely you will have washed your hair.' Harry paused for effect. George Malone said nothing.

'So, anything you would like to say?' Harry asked, with raised eyebrows. Just then there was a knock at the door. 'Come in,' said Harry. A young technician in a white coat entered.

'Thought you would wish to see this immediately, sir,' she said.

Harry took the sheet of paper she offered and said, 'Thank you.' The woman left.

Harry and James read the words on the paper. James tutted, 'Oh dear, this is bad, very bad,' he shook his head.

'Proves I am innocent, does it?' George grinned.

'On the contrary, George Malone,' said Harry, 'it shows a great deal of gunshot residue in your hair and on your clothes. Clothes you did not bother to dispose of.'

George just shrugged, 'It means nothing...absolutely nothing, officer.'

'Maybe you should have disposed of them,' James said.

'No need. It must be from a previous bit of gunfire.' He paused. 'You see, I was shooting at clay pigeons two days ago, me and my mates. I was wearing those same togs. Must be from then.' He smirked.

Harry paused before replying just to let Malone think he had won. 'Unfortunately for you, there is a difference between gunshot residue from a shotgun and that from a pistol.'

'Can't be!' George exclaimed, looking extremely worried.

Harry was bluffing but he persisted along that line, for he had no idea if there was a difference. 'We have you and Sid Malone dead to rights. You may as well admit it and maybe save yourself a few years in prison.'

'I'm admitting to nothing, copper. Me, Sid and Jake Harvey are innocent. We were at…' he was glad they had arranged a story '…the football down the park this morning, weren't we? Nowhere near a bank.' He smirked, hoping the others would not say something else.

'Hmm,' said Harry, 'I'll check Sid's story, shall I?'

'Please yourself. I am innocent. I'm not responsible for anything someone else may have done. Can I go now?' He went to stand up.

'Just stay seated. James, go and find out what Sid has said.'

'Sure thing, Harry,' James Kavenagh replied. He left the room.

Harry said, 'For the tape, DI Kavenagh has left the room. Now, just relax a moment until he returns.' George Malone was wound up tighter than a clock spring but avoided showing it.

Presently, James returned.

'For the tape, DI Kavenagh has resumed his place,' said Harry. 'Now, we shall hear Sid's version'

James spoke, 'Your cousin has said that you two were down at the park this morning. Shame you got your story straight.' He looked George in the eyes.

'I told you we went to the park. There was a match going on. Just some local lads having a friendly kickabout. A young lad named Wilf was a bit handy. Some club should sign him. The new Messi, he is.' George was inventing this as he spoke. There was likely to be a Wilf if the cops checked. He could always say he had misheard the name.

'Very interesting fairy tale, I'm sure, George. Why, not tell us the truth? By the way, who is the other bloke with you in the bank? It was not Harvey, he's too short and wrong hair colour, so what's his name?' James asked and raised his eyebrows awaiting an answer.

'What other bloke? Don't know who you mean. I want a solicitor,' said George and he folded his arms.

'Very well, interview suspended, at 15:30,' Harry said. They were getting nowhere fast.

I went down the corridor to find out what else Sid Malone had said.

Denison had questioned him. 'He has not said a lot. Maintains it was not him in the photo. I doubt if identifying him with a mask on would be convincing in court. His solicitor found it rather amusing.'

'Hmm, what did he use as an alibi?' I asked.

'Well, like I said earlier, he claims they were at some football kickabout.'

'They have made up this alibi. I know they are lying. A gut instinct.' My instincts are rarely wrong.

Denison said, 'Probably, but it is going to be difficult to disprove. The kids would hardly remember them, and in that area of town may not be keen to help the police.'

'Okay,' I said, 'we'll have to let them go. We don't have enough evidence to go to court. I am sure they will slip up sooner or later.' I indicated to the others to let the Malones go.

George and Sid Malone were jubilant about being freed. They went back to George's home with Harvey. He had answered, 'No comment' to all the questions we had asked.

Denison drove home where the cat, in her usual manner, did not welcome him. She just looked up from the rug in front of the fire, verified it was him and then went back to sleep.

His wife was having a nap upstairs. When she came down, she asked how the questioning had gone.

'Not well, to be honest,' Denison replied. 'They had an alibi concocted. George Malone said he had been shooting clay pigeons a few days before, which accounted for the gunshot residue on his clothes. Jacob checked with the Burton and District Clay Pigeon Association and verified that the two Malones and Harvey had indeed been there.'

'Hmm, that's a pity. They must be the luckiest trio in the county.'

Chapter 18
Do You Think You Are Al Capone?

'Great show, lads,' said Sid Malone, gloating. 'The cops could get nothing on us. Imagine trying to prove it was us with a photo of my eyes.' They laughed. 'Sorry, someone's eyes,' he chuckled.

'Yeah, they just looked stupid. Why was Denison there anyway?' asked Jake Harvey. 'Silly old duffer should be at home with his feet up, not still playing detective.' The others agreed.

'Well, we are free,' said George Malone. 'No one mentioned Dave, I hope!' Sid and Harvey shook their heads. 'So, what happens now? Shall we lie low for a while or pull another job?'

'Better give it a few weeks anyway,' Harvey suggested.

'Yes, don't want to push our luck, do we?' Sid added.

'Then, I propose we adjourn to the "White Hart", they have nice outside seating, for a few bevvies,' George said. 'Sid's paying!'

'Why me?' Sid looked annoyed. 'Anyone would think I was a Premiership footballer, rolling in money.' He laughed.

'Not with that belly!' Harvey said, laughing.

'Nothing wrong with my belly. Fit as a twenty-year-old, me,' declared Sid.

In a quiet corner of the pub's terrace, they began to discuss another robbery.

'I think banks are too risky these days. We were nearly done for that last one,' said Harvey.

Sid added, 'Yeah, some prat had to bring a loaded gun!' He glared at George.

'You can blame Dave Smith for that. Anyway, what else can we rob?' George asked.

Harvey began, 'Well…there's security vans, post offices, trains—'

'Do you think you are Al Capone or someone, or Billy the Kid?' Sid looked sceptical.

Harvey shrugged. 'Just thinking out loud, is all.'

The barmaid arrived with their drinks. 'That'll be fourteen pounds sixty-five pence please, luv,' she said holding out a hand.

'Cor, daylight robbery, innit?' Sid groaned. He handed over a twenty-pound note. The barmaid grabbed the money and flounced away. 'And I'm only paying for one round at these prices.' Sid looked determined.

'There's an idea,' joked George. 'Start a pub and fleece people legally.' He laughed.

Harvey laughed and said, 'Only problem, the law would never grant a licence to ex-cons like us.'

'Getting back to serious talk, what can we hit next?' said Sid. The barmaid returned with his change.

'You're a pretty lass, isn't you?' Sid said to her. 'You doing anything later, luv?'

'Yeah, plenty, an' it don't involve an old codger like you!' She turned on her heel and sashayed back to the bar. The other two men roared with laughter. Some other patrons, who overheard the exchange, laughed too. Sid went beetroot with embarrassment. No woman had ever called him an "old codger" before. It offended his ego. His companions grinned.

'Okay, that'll do. We need ideas.' Sid turned serious. 'What can we rob without using guns?'

Harvey said, 'It would need to be at night. Daylight robbery is impossible without guns.'

'Unless you own an oil company. They commit daylight robbery all the time!' George laughed.

'Hmm, very funny,' said Harvey. 'Be serious, George. We need a bank or something which is easy to get into. In and out in a short period of time.'

'Yeah, Jake is right. But where? All the banks have cameras, alarms and stuff galore. It's nearly impossible to rob them without being caught,' said Sid.

'We will need to give it a lot of thought, that's all. Other guys rob banks all the time,' Harvey said.

'Okay, let's think about it and scout around some towns,' Harvey said. 'Little towns where not much happens.'

'Some chance. All the banks are closing local branches every day,' George replied. 'About forty-five a month according to the radio.'

'I'm hungry,' said Sid. 'Let's eat!' He signalled to the waitress.

On his next visit to my office—regular visits were the norm now—Denison said, 'Those three have been very quiet recently. I wonder what they are planning.'

'I assume you mean the Malones and Harvey,' I replied. 'The longer they remain quiet, the better.'

'Yes, those three. I do not think they will retire from crime. Too much easy money to be had in their eyes. I have some snitches on the lookout for information. There is always loose talk in pubs when customers have had a few.' Denison sat back and nodded sagely.

'Would anyone dare to grass on those three? People know their reputations,' I said.

Denison grunted in reluctant agreement.

'Any news about the Malone gang, Walter?' his wife asked.

'Not a lot. Still, early days,' Denison replied.'

'You'll get a lead soon, I'm sure,' Millicent said.

'You are quite right, my Dear. They will slip up sooner or later…preferably sooner,' Denison said. 'What's for tea? I'm starving.'

Millicent grimaced. 'It's a diet you need, Walter Denison, not a big feed.' Denison shrugged. She continued, 'I'll do egg and chips.'

'And baked beans?' Denison added eagerly.

'You'll turn into a baked bean one of these days,' Millicent replied with a laugh.

'Wouldn't bother me, as long as there is plenty of tomato sauce.' Denison grinned.

Chapter 19
Why Has This Bank Not Been
Done Over Before?

'Okay, I have decided to pull a new job,' Sid Malone said to George, Jake Harvey and Dave Smith. 'There's a bank in Belmont on Trent just ripe for plucking.'

Harvey asked, 'Have you checked it out recently, Sid?'

'Yes, two days ago. It's in a quiet street, no security guards and only one camera that I could see. A couple of old dears on the counter. Look like a mouse would scare them. So, no guns, Dave!' He glared at Dave Smith. 'We don't want them having heart attacks.'

Dave looked sceptical. 'Are you just going to ask, "Please can we have all your cash?" Just suppose they don't scare?'

'Obviously, we pretend to have guns in our pockets. We wear overcoats. That will scare them, no problem.' Sid grinned.

'Hmm, sounds too good to be true,' commented George.

'What? You want it to be difficult?' Sid asked, getting annoyed.

'Okay, keep your hair on, cousin. I'm just wondering what we do if things don't go according to plan,' George said. 'Plan A or plan B?'

'Yeah, why has this bank not been done over before?' asked Dave. 'Is there something, some security, not obviously visible?'

Sid said, 'Well, of course it is possible, but unlikely. It is just a quiet town. Most of us bank robbers tend to hit large banks in large cities, don't we?' The others nodded. 'Well, that is the probable reason, so no one will be expecting us.'

The other three sat thinking for a few minutes.

'Well?' Sid asked. He looked from one to the other.

'I'm in,' said George.

'And me,' said Jake Harvey.

'Okay, me too,' said Dave. 'And no real shooters.'

'As someone said, *All for one and one for all*,' Sid declared. They all did high fives in a pact.

'Was that the Telly Tubbies?' Harvey innocently asked. The others laughed.

Later that day in another borrowed car, the four of them arrived in Belmont on Trent and parked in a quiet side street. There were very few people out and about.

'This place is dead,' muttered Harvey. 'Do you think the bank here will be worth robbing, Sid? It's sort of…quiet.'

'Course it will. Trust me. All the rich farmers hereabouts put their money in it. Must be millions of pounds in there, just waiting for new owners!' He laughed. The others were sceptical.

'Hmm, don't know about that, mate. Farmers are always claiming to be skint, penniless,' said George. Dave and Harvey agreed.

'Just wait and see,' said Sid. 'Now, as soon as we get to the bank, masks on, a hand in a pocket as if we had guns and hey presto, loads of lolly.'

'Jake, have the car ready for a quick getaway.'

'Yep, I'll pull over in front of the bank when you guys go in,' Harvey replied.

Sid, George and Dave strolled casually towards the bank. They were about one hundred feet away when Police Constable Potts, on his beat, came round a corner. He was in a jovial mood.

Sid spoke out of the side of his mouth, 'Just keep walking, lads.' All three walked on past the bank. Potts stopped in front of the bank and chatted with someone he knew. He knew just about everyone in the town. A bit like the old TV character "Dixon of Dock Green".

'Oh, good morning, Mrs Carruthers, isn't it a lovely day?' he said, smiling broadly.

'Yes, it is indeed, Mr Potts. I was just getting something for my Harry's dinner. Very partial to a nice piece of steak is Harry.'

'Can't say as I would turn down a nice steak, with onions, myself, Mrs C. Give Harry my best wishes, I must be off on my rounds,' said Potts and he touched his helmet in salute and strolled on.

What a nice man is Mr Potts, Mrs Carruthers thought.

Sid and his companions stopped walking when they saw Potts leaving.

'Thank goodness that copper is leaving. Right, lads, back we go, and remember to act casual until we get into the bank,' said Sid.

'Okay,' the others said in unison. Dave lived up to his nickname "Accident Prone" and tripped on a paving stone. *That's right, draw attention to us, why don't you,* Sid thought. Passers-by were all looking.

Harvey had also seen PC Potts and driven on and then turned back the way he came. He pulled into a space in front of the bank just as the others entered.

'Stay where you are. This is a robbery,' Sid shouted. They had put on masks as they came through the door.

The staff, Miss Dorothy Smythe, mid-fifties, tall, face like a bulldog chewing a wasp, and Mr Wilbur Jones, skinny, bald and probably scared of spiders, stopped what they were doing. The few customers did likewise.

'What is the meaning of this?' Miss Smythe demanded to know. 'How dare you come in here scaring people?'

'Er, just put your hands up, lady,' said Sid. He thought, *Why are bank ladies so cantankerous?*

'I demand that you leave immediately,' she replied. She had dealt with robbers before.

'Shut up, missus,' said Dave pointing his coat pocket at her by way of having a gun.

'You rude, impudent scoundrel,' Miss Smythe replied looking extremely angry. (Make that a bulldog chewing a handful of wasps.) 'I am a miss and I will not shut up. Now, get out! And do not think for one minute your hand in a pocket fools me.'

The three men were stunned. They did not know what to do. They had not been prepared for this. They looked at each other.

Miss Smythe shouted, 'And I have pressed the alarm. The police will be here in moments.'

Then Sid shrugged, 'Come on, lads, let's go. This is a waste of time.' They all rushed out to the car...only there was no car. A traffic warden had spotted Harvey parked on a double yellow line and insisted he move!

'What! Where? Where's Harvey?' George shouted, looking around.

'Run for it,' Sid said and ran back to the side street where they had been. The other two followed. No sign of Harvey. What to do? Just then Harvey pulled up and they bundled in. Harvey sped off back to their hometown. After dumping the car, they went to the Malones' house.

After they got their breath back, Sid said, 'What a fiasco. Boy, can we pick 'em. What an old battleaxe she was!' They all sat for a few moments then burst out laughing.

George said, 'You got to laugh. She was something else. Like in one of these *Carry On* films.'

Dave added, 'Scary or what?'

'Where did you get to, by the way?' Sid asked Jake Harvey.

'Got moved on by a traffic warden, didn't I? Said he would call a cop if I didn't. There was a PC up the street.'

'Why do we always get hassle? Other guys rob banks with no problem. Us? We get hassle. Where do they get those women bank clerks? Like female Genghis Khans they are,' George said. 'They must have a training school: "Gorgons are Us".'

'Hmm, never mind. Put it down to experience,' Sid said, and they laughed again.

'Right, what do we try next?' Sid continued.

'Somewhere where there are no people. Middle of the night is better,' said Dave Smith.

'I agree,' said Harvey. So, they agreed on no more daytime robberies.

Denison read in the Castlewood News and Advertiser newspaper next morning, over breakfast, of the thwarted robbery in Belmont on Trent: "Three masked and apparently armed robbers attempted to hold up the bank in Belmont on Trent, Staffordshire, yesterday, Wednesday. Eyewitnesses agreed that they were scared off by the bravery of staff member Miss Dorothy Smythe. The robbers, it seems, pretended to have guns in their overcoat pockets".

'Darling, read that.' He handed the paper to his wife. She read the article.

'Do you think it is the Malone gang, Walter?'

'I'd bet my last dollar on it if I had any dollars,' he replied. 'It's the sort of idiotic antic they would do. Guns in their pockets! Sounds like a Morecambe and Wise sketch.'

'Or The Two Ronnies,' his wife replied.

He phoned me later. 'Jacob,' he said, 'I've just been reading about a bank robbery—'

'In Belmont, yes I know. We suspect our old friends, the Malones. Some of the lads are going to have a word with them as we speak.'

'Exactly what I was thinking,' Denison said. 'Let me know what they say, will you?'

'I certainly will, old chap. Now, I had better dash…meeting the Chief Constable in five mins. Bye'

DS Daniel Parker and DS Mary Freeman called at 57, Crew Lane, the Malone residence. Residence might be a bit grand for it was a rather rundown, semi-detached house.

George shouted to Sid, 'Hey, there's two people getting out of a car. They look like cops, Sid!'

'Do not panic, they have nothing on us. No one saw our faces so they are only trying to scare us,' Sid replied.

George opened the front door a fraction.

'Mr George Malone?' DS Freeman asked as she showed her warrant card.

'Yep, that's me,' George replied.

'I am Detective Sergeant Freeman from Castlewood CID, and this is Detective Sergeant Parker. We would like to ask you and Sidney Malone a few questions. May we come in?' She was ready to put her foot in the door if he refused.

'Yeah sure, officers. We've nothing to hide. You'll have to excuse the mess. It's Sid's day for cleaning and tidying. Need I say more?' Sid made a disapproving face.

Sid asked, 'Well, what are we supposed to have done now?' He didn't bother to stand.

DS Parker said, 'There has been an attempted robbery at a local bank, in Belmont. You pair would not happen to know anything about it, I suppose?'

'Us!' exclaimed George looking aggrieved. 'We have been here all day. Never left, have we, Sid?'

'Nope, never left. Not for a minute, officer. We have no transport. If we had robbed a bank, we would not have failed. We are, what you might call, professionals, though we are retired, so to speak, I hasten to add. Strictly law-abiding citizens we are.' Sid smiled like the Cheshire Cat.

'Was it Jake Harvey who was driving?' DS Freeman asked. 'An eyewitness described a man in a car outside the bank. Parked on a double yellow line, he was.'

DS Parker added, 'Fits your pal Harvey to a T. So, can you explain why he was outside a bank in Belmont while three men were robbing it, possibly, or probably, you two and another?'

'Dunno, guv. You should ask Jake. Sorry, we cannot assist you. We would if we could, but we can't,' said George. He grinned.

'He is being apprehended as we speak,' DS Parker replied. 'We shall be seeing you again, no doubt. Don't leave the country.' The two detectives went back to their car.

Jake Harvey was likewise questioned.

'I have been here all day, officers,' he told DS Robin Sanderson and DS Kelvin Grant.

'A witness described the driver of a getaway car parked outside a bank, while it was being robbed. The description matches you, Mr Harvey,' Kelvin said.

'*Moi?* Impossible! I must have a double.' Harvey grinned. 'They do say that everyone has a double, don't they?'

'Nevertheless, I must ask you to accompany us to the station for questioning,' Kelvin continued.

'Okay, if I must. But you are wasting your time.'

At the police station, Harvey sat opposite the two detectives.

'Now, as I said earlier, Harvey, you were described as being the driver of a vehicle outside the bank. Said vehicle having been stolen as it turns out,' said Kelvin.

'And like I said, officer, I was at home. Watching the cricket as it happens. And before you ask, I have no witnesses. My cousin Tom, that's Tom Paton, was out doing something or other. I was alone, minus company, on my tod, *sans amis* as the French say.'

'The car you were driving...' Kelvin held up a hand to stop Harvey's protest, '...is being forensically tested at this very moment. If we find so much as a hair of yours, you will be nicked.'

Harvey shook his head. He was suddenly extremely worried. 'I was not involved in any robbery. I am not going back to prison, so I'm going straight. My cousin, Tom, would kick me out of the house if I did robberies and such. Very law-abiding is Tom.'

Kelvin and Robin consulted me on how to proceed.

I said, 'Until we get forensics from the car, we have no evidence. Let him go for the moment but have him followed. He was in it with the Malones and another bloke, I'm sure of it. The Malones are being followed if they leave the house. We'll see if they contact that guy, then we lift him for questioning.'

'Okay, boss,' the two detectives said in unison and left.

Harvey later went to the Malones' house and the three went down to the pub. Dave Smith joined them about thirty minutes later. They did not notice a young couple some fifteen metres away who seemed to be deep in a romantic conversation. They were really DC Jack Longworth and DC Julie Andrews, named after the famous actress. Her mother, Sylvia Andrews, loved "The Sound of Music".

Dave Smith looked around the room but saw nothing suspicious. He said, 'Well, lads, did you manage to throw the fuzz off the track?'

'Yeah, we did,' Sid replied.

'Okay,' said Dave, 'what do we do now?'

'Perhaps we should go back to breaking in the backway as we had planned before?' said Harvey.

'Hmm, we could. But a different bank. There is no way we could get in that one with all those cameras and security guards,' said Sid Malone.

The two detectives were leaning across their table being all lovey-dovey but holding a microphone in their hands. It was pointing at the Malone gang.

DC Longworth whispered, 'They are planning a robbery!' DC Andrews grinned.

'Okay, we try another. Loads of banks around…at least those that have not been closed,' Harvey said, laughing.

'What about the one we hit in Burton years ago?' Sid suggested.

'Worth a try. We could scout it out tomorrow. See what's what, anyway,' Harvey agreed.

'Great, tomorrow it is, lads,' said Dave. Now, drink up. Whose round is it?'

'Yours!' the others said as one.

'It would be!' Dave sighed and went to the bar.

The two cops slipped out, arms entwined, till they reached their car. Andrews phoned me at home.

'Boss, good news,' she said jubilantly.

'It had better be,' I laughed, 'at this time of night.'

'There are four of them: the two Malones, Harvey and another bloke. I didn't recognise him but Jack thinks he is David Smith, a small-time crook. They are going to case a bank in Burton tomorrow. Sid Malone said something about having hit it before. Does that ring a bell?'

'Oh, great news. A bank in Burton! Let me think,' I said. 'Oh yes, I remember in their file; they robbed one just before we nabbed them for some murders. We'll have it watched.

Great work, you two. I'll say goodnight. I am completely exhausted.'

'Goodnight, sir,' DC Andrews said, and gave her companion a high five.

'Now, where were we?' DC Longworth said, grinning hopefully. He had always fancied Andrews.

'You can forget that, Jack Longworth. You are not my type,' she replied, laughing. 'Besides, I have a husband and two kids.'

'Can't blame a guy for trying.' Jack grinned.

Chapter 20
The Bank in Burton upon Trent

Next morning, the four robbers borrowed another car and drove to Burton upon Trent.

'That's it there,' Sid said, pointing at their target, The Burton Savings and Investment Bank Ltd. It was an imposing edifice at the front: a flight of granite steps led up to a portico with four sturdy pillars with Doric capitals, and a pediment decorated with allegorical figures of Thrift, Industry, Wealth, Plenty and Progress, also carved in granite. Wealth had unfortunately lost her bag of gold due to a drunk throwing a beer bottle at her!

'Wow, that's some joint, guys,' drawled Dave Smith. He watched a lot of American gangster movies.

'Okay, let's wander around to the back gate and see what's what,' Sid said. 'One at a time so as not to look suspicious. If anyone asks what we are doing, try the missing dog routine.' The others nodded.

One by one, they walked down an alley to the back of the bank.

Harvey said, in a low voice, 'Sid, it has hardly changed a bit. Some new razor wire, a few new cameras and that's it!'

Sid grinned from ear to ear, or what remained of his right ear which had been bitten off in a fight when he was a teenager. 'Yeah, should be a piece of cake. I take out the cameras with my catapult like before, then Dave picks the lock on the gate and Bob's your uncle, we're in. I'll need to practice a bit first. I haven't used my catty in years.'

Dave said, 'That lock looks easy. I cannot believe their security is so poor.'

Back in their car, they discussed the robbery. Sid Malone said, 'Should not be too difficult. Pity there are no football matches on which we could use as a distraction. We arranged a riot to keep the cops busy, didn't we, Jake?'

'Sure did. It worked a treat,' Jake Harvey replied. The other two men grinned.

'Maybe a wee bit of arson somewhere to cause confusion?' George Malone suggested, raising an eyebrow.

'Good idea. The other side of town. Right, when to carry this out?' Sid asked.

Dave looked up something on his mobile phone. 'Going to be a cloudy, moonless night on the…sixteenth. Three days from now!'

'Perfect. Okay, head back home, Jake,' Sid said. Harvey started the engine and headed back to Castlewood.

'Right, where's my trusty catapult?' Sid said as he searched through some drawers.

'I put it somewhere when you went into the nick,' George said. 'Can't for the life of me remember where.'

Sid shouted triumphantly, 'Ah, here it is!' He held up the item in question. 'Hmm, needs a new rubber band. Anyone got an old bicycle inner tube handy?'

'There's that old bike in the garden shed. Not ridden in years…needed a new saddle,' George said with a laugh. 'Bit sore on the posterior otherwise.'

'Okay, I'll have a look. Then do a bit of practice in the garden,' Sid said, and he went out through the back door.

An hour later, the neighbours were wondering why a middle-aged man was firing at some tin cans!

'It is great,' Sid said in triumph. 'I haven't lost my touch. Ten hits out of ten! We are set to go.'

'Right,' Dave Smith said, 'we will need masks and rubber gloves. I checked and there is no way of knocking off the electricity so the CCTV will be working.'

'And woollen hats so we don't leave any stray hairs,' Jake Harvey added.

'All sorted,' George said. 'I spoke to Billy Grundy, a mate, on the phone and he will bring the gear round this afternoon.'

'Excellent! Then roll on the sixteenth,' said Sid.

The night arrived. Grundy had agreed to start a blaze at the Pirelli Stadium, home of Burton Albion F.C. Every firefighter in town and most of the cops were called out.

The Malone gang gathered at the back gate of the bank. Sid quickly took out the cameras and lights in the yard with his catapult firing ball bearings, as Dave opened the padlock on the gate. They hurried across the yard to the rear door of the bank. Again, Dave made short work of the lock on the door.

'This is too easy,' Sid said, looking worried.

'Don't knock it, mate. Easier the better,' Dave said as the four of them headed for the room with the safe. They entered only to find the safe door open and the contents gone!

'Some rotten swine has beaten us to it,' Harvey said, unnecessarily.

'All that work for nothing,' Sid added with a sigh. 'Come on, let's get out of here before—'

'Stay where you are. This is the police.' A voice with a megaphone made them all freeze.

'The cops!' cried Harvey. 'They must have been tipped off.'

Sid exclaimed, 'Yeah, some lowlife has tipped them off. Okay, this is our story: we were walking past the gate, it was open and being good citizens, we investigated and we found the safe empty. Got that?' The others nodded. 'Dump your masks and gloves in that bin, under the rubbish.' He also dumped the catapult. He hoped the police would not search the room.

Moments later, a dozen cops rushed in through the rear door. I was leading them. We had had a tip-off from a snitch in Burton who had heard of the fire being a decoy. Best two hundred pounds we had ever spent.

'So, we meet again, gentlemen,' I said. 'Sidney and George Malone and Jacob Harvey and another, whom I have never met. What is your name, sir?' I asked with great sarcasm.

'Er, David Smith, Dave to me mates,' Dave replied. 'We were just passing and saw—'

'Save it for the court. I have not come across you before. I am sure you will have a criminal record, nonetheless. Constables, take them away.'

The four were led out, handcuffed, and herded into a police van, protesting about their treatment.

The next morning at nine a.m. we began the interrogations. DI Harry Trevelyan and I took Sid Malone; DI James Kavenagh and DS Mary Freeman took George Malone, and Robin Sanderson, Dan Parker and Kelvin Grant took Harvey and Smith in turn.

'Interview with Sidney Malone. Also present is his solicitor, Clarence Buckingham, DI Harry Trevelyan and me, DCS Jacob Marley.'

'Mr Malone, you and three others were apprehended yesterday the 23rd of August on the premises of The Burton Savings and Investment Bank Ltd. in Burton upon Trent, Staffordshire. Have you anything to say?'

'Aye, plenty. We were just passing by and saw the gate and back door open, so, being good citizens, like, we decided to have a butcher's and found the safe empty.' Sid smiled innocently.

'For the benefit of the tape, explain "having a butcher's" please,' I said.

'That's butcher's hook, as in look, rhyming slang for the uninitiated. Then you lot barged in.'

'You just happened to be passing by! All four of you, in the dark, in Burton? Don't talk nonsense. I wasn't born yesterday. You robbed the bank and passed the proceeds to another who scarpered with it. Is that not the case?' I asked. I was shaking my head slowly.

'It's true, I swear. No law against having a walk! The safe was empty. The real robbers had legged it already. We were just being concerned citizens. Straight up, officer. No lie.'

Harry leaned over and whispered in my ear, 'We can compare this tale with what the others say, sir.' I nodded.

'Who did you pass the loot to? If it is recovered intact, it might go in your favour in court,' I said.

'I repeat, I do not know. The safe was empty when we arrived...to investigate. Someone had been and gone like I said before. G-O-N-E as in no longer there.'

'Okay, constable, take him back to this cell, please,' I said to a constable by the door.

'Yes, sir,' he said. Sid was led away.

'Interview with George Malone. Also present DS Mary Freeman and DI James Kavenagh,' said James.

'Mr George Malone, when you and your gang were arrested in the bank, The Burton Savings and Investment Bank Ltd., what had you done with the cash in the safe?' Mary asked.

George Malone replied, 'I never saw no cash, officer. The safe was empty when we...when we got there.'

'You were about to say when we opened the safe, weren't you?'

'No, I was not. When we got in, we saw the safe open. I do not know why it was empty. Some thief must have been and gone. Legged it with our, er, the money.'

'Why were the four of you in the bank?' James asked.

George had been trying to remember the reason, which Sid had said, for being in the bank. He tried to sound as if it was a common occurrence to be in a bank after closing time.

'We were just passing by and saw the gate and the door open so, just out of curiosity, we kind of wandered in, like you do. Thought it odd, it being open, like, and then we saw the empty safe. Hello, I thought, that's odd. That should be locked. I said so to the others. Then your lot arrived before we could call the police. So, that's about it, officer.' *Try to prove otherwise,* he thought.

'And then there was Goldilocks and the three bears! Do you really think we will believe that fairy tale? You robbed the bank and got someone else to make off with the cash, but you stayed a bit too long and were nicked,' James Kavenagh said, shaking his head. 'DS Freeman, have you ever heard a yarn like that before?'

'No, I never did, sir. Great imagination he has, that's for sure. He would give Jeffrey Archer competition,' DS Mary Freeman replied.

DI Kavenagh said, 'Constable, take him back to a cell.' The constable standing by the door took George away.

James said to Mary, 'We'll compare that to what the others have said.'

(Unknown to the police at the time, the bank manager, Wilberforce Pettigrew had seized the opportunity, when warned of a robbery being carried out that night, to fill bags with cash. He packed a suitcase and his passport and he headed for the airport. Destination unknown…but that, as they say, is another story.)

'Interview with Jacob Harvey. Also present DS Daniel Parker, DS Kelvin Grant, and DS Robin Sanderson,' Robin said.

'Why were you and your pals in the bank, The Burton Savings and Investment Bank Ltd?' Kelvin asked.

'Just passing by, weren't we? The gate and door were open and we went in to check it out, as you do. We found the open safe and the cash gone.' Harvey tried to look unconcerned.

'Come on, admit it, lad. You were on the rob and passed the cash to an accomplice, didn't you?' Kelvin said.

'Nope, we were just passing by. Not our fault if the bank has no security, is it?'

'Four of you, from Castlewood, were "just passing by" the bank in Burton, at night, in an alley. Pull the other one, it's got bells on,' Kelvin said. The three detectives shook their heads.

'It's the truth, so it is. Minding our own business, we were. Last time I will try to do a favour, that's for sure. No gratitude some people. I ask you. Tsk!' He tutted.

'Why, exactly, were the four of you walking in an alley, behind a bank, in Burton and late at night?' Robin asked.

'We just fancied some fresh air, innit? No law says you have to do that in your own town, is there? Free country…or it used to be.' Harvey sat back with a satisfied smirk on his face.

'Right, back to your cell, pending further enquiries. Constable, lock him up,' Kelvin said. He knew that Harvey was lying through his teeth but needed proof.

'Interview with David Stanley Smith. Also present DS Robin Sanderson, DS Kelvin Grant, and DS Daniel Parker,' Daniel said for the tape.

'Why were you and your pals in the bank, The Burton Savings and Investment Bank Ltd?' Kelvin asked.

Dave was not the brightest of guys so he thought before he answered. *What had Sid said?*

'We was just passing the bank so we was, and we saw the gate open. The back door was open too. So, just to be nosy, like, we went in. There was nobody about and then we saw the empty safe. Then the boys in blue arrived before we could dial 999. That's about it, officers.' Dave was quite pleased with himself and folded his arms across his chest. He found it difficult to remember things.

Kelvin glanced at Dan and Robin to see if they had noticed. Robin's eyes were wide as saucers. Sitting in front of them was a bloke with only three fingers on his right hand! 'Interview suspended,' Kelvin said. Dave thought he had beaten them and smiled.

Kelvin left the room and went to where I had resumed interviewing Sid Malone.

'Sorry to disturb you, sir, but something has come up,' Kelvin said.

I stood up and made for the door. 'Interview suspended,' I said as I walked.

Once in the corridor, I said, sharply, 'This had better be good, Kelvin.'

'This'll blow your socks off, sir,' he replied, grinning.

'Don't just stand there grinning, man. Out with it,' I growled.

'David Smith has a finger missing…the little finger…on his right hand!'

I was almost speechless. 'An actual finger missing? Brilliant! We may be able to link the four of them to the murder of Mulgrew. And the six murders decades ago. Good work, Kelvin.' I was like a dog with two tails. 'Compare his fingerprints, the remaining ones, and DNA, to the handprint in the car.'

I returned to the interview with Sid Malone. 'Well now, Mr Malone, it appears your friend, Smith, may well be linked to a murder a few months ago. You would not happen to know anything about that, would you?'

'A few months ago? That would have been while I was in prison, would it not? So, the answer is no, I know nothing about a murder.' He looked smug. I wanted to wipe that smugness off his face.

'The victim of said murder was Fred Mulgrew, a relative of a Mulgrew murdered some twenty years ago. I'm sure you know whom I mean.' Sid shook his head and shrugged. 'Well, I intend to make the connection, Malone, so don't expect to be a free man again. Interview ended.' As I spoke, another constable arrived.

'Sir, guess what they have found in the bank?' she said.

'No idea. Why don't you just tell me?' I was in a bad mood.

'Only found four masks and four pairs of rubber gloves, and a catapult, would you believe, hidden in a bin.' She grinned.

'Great. Get them tested for DNA immediately. Top priority, urgent, *pronto, immediatment*,' I said feeling jubilant.

'Will do, sir.' She hurried off.

I went back to the interview. 'Interview resumed. Sit down, Malone,' I said. Harry Trevelyan switched the tape back on.

'It seems you and your companions did not hide your burgling equipment very well. Namely, masks and gloves and a catapult.' Sid tried to look unconcerned. 'They were found in a bin where you lot had stashed them. Why were you wearing them when out for a walk? They are being tested for DNA, so don't bother lying.'

'Er,' Sid hesitated. 'We did not want to contaminate the crime scene so we put on the gloves, We watch all those cop dramas on the television, don't we?' He grinned.

'Just accidentally happened to have four pairs of rubber gloves, not to mention the masks! Do we look like mugs to you, Mr Malone? Or should we call you Hans Christian Andersen?'

'I couldn't possibly say, officer.' Sid smiled benignly. He had not a clue who Andersen was.

'And the masks?'

'It was a chilly night. What can I say?' Sid replied.

'Who owned the catapult?' I asked forcefully. Sid just shrugged.

'As I said, they are being tested as we speak. You will remain in custody until we get a result. Take him away, Harry.'

I then went to the interview with Dave Smith.

Kelvin said, 'For the tape, DCS Marley has entered the room.'

I sat down and asked, 'I have just been informed of your missing digit, Smith.' I indicated his right hand.

'What of it? Had an accident is all,' he replied. 'Accident prone, me.'

'Well, we have been searching for a person who is lacking a little finger, in connection with the murder of a chap named Fred Mulgrew.' Smith looked pale when he heard this. 'We are, of course, checking your fingerprints against those on a blood smear in a crashed car. I am sure they will match.' I paused.

'I got no connection to no murder, detective. I never heard of this Fred Whatshisname,' Smith said.

I was not convinced. 'Interview suspended.'

A few days later, the DNA results arrived in my office.

'Right then, the DNA shows the stuff found in the bank belongs, without a doubt, to our four suspects. The fingerprints in the crashed car are David Smith's, aka three-finger-guy,' I said to the staff.

DI Harry Trevelyan said, 'A nice, neat link between Smith, the murder of Mulgrew, and Harvey and the Malones. We just need a confession from Smith or more conclusive links.'

'Harvey and the Malones! Sounds like a pop group,' said Robin.

I got Sid Malone back in the interview room for questioning.

'Sidney Malone, there is now proof that your pal, Smith, is linked to the recent killing of Fred Mulgrew, which also provides a link to the Mulgrew, one of the six murdered some twenty years ago. Anything you want to say about that?' I asked.

He consulted his solicitor who shook his head. 'I have got nothing to say 'bout that, officer,' Sid said. 'And even if I did, I am not a grass.'

'You can save yourself a lot of prison time if you own up and plead guilty,' I urged.

'Yeah, I know, but I'm not a grass. I don't go telling the cops about people. That's informing. I have never informed in my life. You and I know what happens to informers.' He raised an eyebrow.

'Yes, we know that, Malone. We suspect you were behind those multiple killings twenty years ago, and a conviction would see you put away for the rest of your natural.'

'That had nothing to do with me or Jake Harvey. We were still in the clink when that happened. You can't go pinning all sorts on us.' Malone folded his arms decisively.

'Must have been George Malone then,' I stated. Sid looked startled.

'It weren't him either. George would not kill someone. Very peaceable bloke is George. Wouldn't even kill a spider what is in his bath.'

'Hmm, that's debatable, Malone. But rest assured, I shall find out,' I said.

'I told you I am not grassing on anyone. I've my reputation to think of. If the guys out there,' he gestured towards the window, 'knew I was a grass, I would be as good as dead.' Malone looked pale.

'Was Smith the one who supplied the guns for the failed robbery?'

'Failed robbery? Guns? Don't know what you are talking 'bout.' Malone folded his arms and sat back.

'You know what robbery. A few more seconds and you all would have been caught red-handed,' I said forcefully.

'Well, we shall leave you in a cell to think about it. Interview suspended.' I stood up and left. Sid was removed to this cell again.

While he was in custody, Smith's flat was searched; Smith was predictably silent, answering, 'No comment' to all my questions. I told him his accomplices had named him as the gun supplier and as the fourth member of the gang. I hoped my bluff would loosen his tongue.

He got angry and stood up putting his hands on the table. I told him to sit down.

'Did you know a chap named Fred Mulgrew?' I threw this out to see his reaction. He looked up.

After a second or two, he said, 'Nah, never heard of him.'

'Murdered recently, shot in the heart. Does that ring a bell, Smith?' I looked intently at him. 'We found a weapon hidden in your flat. Won't take long to match the bullets. Oh, and we need a saliva sample to compare DNA.' Again he looked up, startled.

'Why do you need that? I've never left blood anywhere. Why do you want it?' He was plainly worried. 'And that gun is one I have had for years. It has not been fired in decades.'

'We shall see. Forensics will reveal all. And we need a handprint of your right hand, Smith.' I raised an eyebrow.

'The light suddenly dawned on Smith. He had left a handprint in the crashed car. 'I'm saying no more,' he stated.

'Take him to a cell,' I said to a constable.

I was very pleased with the outcome. I only needed to link the Malones and Harvey with the Mulgrew killing and we were ready for court. Ideally, I sincerely hoped for a link to the historic murder cases as well.

After some days trying to think of a connection—none of the four were prepared to give any information—I telephoned Walter Denison.

'Good morning, Walter, Jacob here, are you still enjoying retirement?' I asked.

'Oh, nice to hear from you. Yes, it's not too bad. Got most of the odd jobs done around the house. The kitten is growing quickly. You would hardly recognise her now.'

'That's nice. I'm pleased you like her—but I have not called just for a chat. The thing is, we have come so far with the Malone case but cannot just get the missing link. Let me bring you up to date. We have a chap, the one with the missing finger, in custody. Evidence proves he was in the car involved with the killing of Fred Mulgrew. He probably was the killer, but what I cannot get is a link to the Malone and Harvey pair. Smith, he is the missing finger bloke, is refusing to grass on them.'

'Not Dave "Accident Prone" Smith?' Denison interrupted.

'Yes, it is. Do you know him?' I asked hopefully. 'Silly question: you obviously do.'

'I certainly do, Jacob. He definitely was around at the time of the six deaths. I don't know if he was linked to Malone and Harvey though. He was interviewed but we could not get conclusive evidence. A woman he knew gave him an alibi for the day in question. Cannot recall what it was just off-hand, and as he had no previous, we let him go. He had all his fingers then though. Or, at least I did not notice one missing.'

'Hmm,' I mused. 'It is really annoying when you know a bloke is a bad un' but you cannot clinch the deal.'

'I know the feeling,' Denison agreed. 'I'll have a think over the past contact and see if anything comes to mind. At my age, it is easy to forget. I'll be in contact soon.'

'Okay, take care,' I said and turned off my phone.

Some days later, Denison called at my office.

'Good morning, Walter,' I said. 'Have you come up with anything useful?'

'Yes, actually I have…I hope. Wally Mulgrew, one of the six victims of the savage massacre, was the brother of the informer who told us where Malone and Harvey were hiding out. The other five were: Markovich, Speers, Williams or Williamson, Bancroft and Leonard. I'll not bother about the first names because I can't remember them.' He chuckled. 'Anyway, all had informed on Malone at some stage. They were fairly hefty lads and spent a lot of time in the gym, so it would have taken a gang to overpower them. Colin Harrison was one member of the murder gang. As you know, he was murdered before he could reveal any names. Sid Malone and Harvey had been in prison for five years or so at that time.'

'How does that help us now, Walter?' I asked. I was getting a bit impatient.

'The only person who was found to have visited both in prison—remember they were in separate establishments— was a bloke named Monty Burnside. He had an alibi for the day of the killings; he was in the nick in Stafford on a drunk and disorderly charge. I thought at the time he could have arranged that deliberately to avoid suspicion. He had no previous record.'

'So, he had others do the dirty work?' I asked.

'Exactly. Now all we need, hopefully, is to find him, if still alive, and get him to finger Malone and Harvey. We can then see a link with the murder of Wally Mulgrew and the recent one of Fred Mulgrew, the brother I mentioned.'

'You make it sound easy. Is this Burnside likely to tell all after so many years? He is bound to have heard what happened to Harrison, and he was only thinking of grassing.'

Chapter 21
DNA

As I was chatting with Denison, there was a knock at the door.

'Enter,' I said. Mary Freeman came in.

'Sorry for interrupting, sir…Oh. Good morning, Mr Denison, how nice to see you, sir.'

'Good to see you too, Mary. Everything well with you?'

'Yes, can't complain,' she replied. I coughed to end the small talk.

'Oh, yes, sir, this is why I'm here,' she continued. 'I just noticed the DNA for this bloke Smith is a very close match to that of Mrs Sugden and her brother Tom Paton.'

'Is it?' I was astonished. 'So, they are related. That's interesting.'

'Very interesting,' Denison said.

'There has never been any mention of a family link, by any of them,' I said.

'Too close a match to be just cousins, sir,' said Mary. 'More like siblings!'

'Hmm, both have said they have no other siblings. Get them both in here again, Mary.'

'Will do, sir.' She left and sent two detectives to round up the pair.

'Now,' I said, 'Mrs Sugden and Mr Paton, this is former Inspector Denison who is aiding this investigation.' Denison nodded as they sat down. 'It has come to light that a person named David Smith has a close, very close, DNA match to yourselves. A familial match as it is known.'

'What?' they exclaimed in unison.

'A match? Impossible,' exclaimed Paton.

'There is no doubt about it. He is being held for the murder of Fred Mulgrew. His blood was tested and, as I said, the DNA is almost identical to yours.' I sat back and waited.

Paton said, after a few moments, 'Is he that shifty-looking bloke my cousin Jake and the Malones are pals with? How could he be our brother and us not know it?'

I replied, 'Half-brother, presumably. Sorry to be blunt. Perhaps he does not know either.'

Mrs Sugden, recovering from the shock, said, 'That means our father was…'

Paton said, 'Let's not go into that, Mary. Inspector, we knew nothing of what the four of them were doing. Malone and Harvey did try to rope me into a job some time ago. I refused 'cause my girlfriend overheard them and gave me an ultimatum, or whatever the word is, so I backed out.'

I said, 'Alright, sorry for springing this on you, but I had to check.

'Do you know if Malone, Harvey or Smith made any mention of Fred Mulgrew in recent days? It is vital we establish a link while Malone was in prison.'

They looked at each other, and then Paton said, 'I heard them mention a Mulgrew, about four or five weeks ago. I just caught the name before they clammed up and changed the subject, Inspector.'

'I don't think we need bother you further,' I said. 'DS Freeman will show you out.'

The two stood and walked out muttering about their father and his other life of which they knew nothing.

'Oh, one quick question,' I asked, 'before you go.' They stopped and looked round. 'To your knowledge, was this Smith around some twenty or twenty-five years ago?'

'I think he was. Yes, he lived nearby. Wasn't a relative back then though,' Paton said. 'I think he was a crony of Malone's back then for sure.'

Mrs Suden added, 'The three of them hung out at the Mad Hatter Pub down by the canal. Come to think of it, our dad was seen there often, too.'

Tom Paton gasped, 'The barmaid, Greta something, had the same hair colour as Smith has!' Brother and sister looked at each other.

'Okay, thanks.' I smiled and they continued on their way.

Paton was grumbling as they walked down the corridor, 'I am going to have words with our dad…'

Denison said, 'Well, that certainly helps to link Malone and Co with Smith back then and hence with the murders, possibly. The problem is how to prove they were behind the six historic murders and the Mulgrew one.'

'I have no idea, Walter. It sounds like what Sherlock Holmes would have called "a three pipe problem", or something to that effect.'

Denison clicked his fingers. 'Speaking of pipes, I left my pipe sitting in the lounge. If the missus finds it, I am sunk, big-time. I had better be off home sharpish.'

I laughed and said goodbye. I had never seen Walter move so quickly!

Chapter 22
A Letter Arrives

I called all the staff in for a conference.

'Right, we need to get some results on the Malone gang,' I said. 'We have Smith for murdering, or at least being an accessory to murdering, Fred Mulgrew. His half-siblings, Mrs Sugden and Tom Paton, say he was around at the time of the six killings twenty years ago but was not known to be related. He had associated with Malone and Harvey before that. Have I missed anything?'

DI Harry Trevelyan said, 'That seems to cover it, boss. But it still does not implicate Harvey and Sid Malone in any of the murders.'

'They were both locked up at the time,' added Mary Freeman.

'Yes, I know,' I said. 'If only we could get Smith to confess, to state they were involved.'

A knock at the door: a detective constable opened it and said, 'Excuse the interruption, sir, but you need to see this.' She handed over a letter in a transparent evidence bag and left.

'Hmm, I wonder what this is…' My jaw dropped when I read the contents. In capital letters cut from a magazine, it read thus: 'TO WHO IT MITE CONCERN I WISH TO GET A GILT OF MY KONSHUNS I WAS ONE OF THE MEN WHAT HELPED DAVE SMITH KILL 6 BLOKES BACK ABOUT 20 YEARS AND THE MULGREW GEEZER MORE RECENT MALONE AND HARVIE WERE THE ONES WHAT WERE BEHIND THEM KILLINGS CANOT GIVE ANY MORE INFO WITH OUT REVEALING MY IDENTATY. Poor English,' I commented.

'Not signed, of course,' I added. The others were amazed and just lost for words.

Robin Sanderson said, 'It shows we are on the right track, at least, sir.'

'But is it reliable?' James Kavenagh asked. 'Could be from some idiot.'

'It won't stand up in court, for sure,' Mary Freeman said.

'Yes, I am sure you are right. But it may give us some leverage on Smith,' I said.

'I assume the writer was with Smith at the killing of Mulgrew, sir. In the car, which would mean Smith would have him or her silenced, given the chance.'

'Yes, we need to tread carefully,' I said. 'If we could get hold of this person, we could obtain the names of the others involved twenty years ago.'

'We could put an advert in the paper asking him, or her, to write again. Totally in confidence, sir,' suggested Robin.

'Yes, in confidence. Good idea, Robin,' I said. 'Worth a try. Could you draft a suitable advert? Keep it vague so Smith or his pals are not alerted. Oh, and have this checked for fingerprints. Probably none but you never know. And someone find which magazine was used for this.'

'Will do, sir,' Robin replied.

'Now we just need to await a reply,' I said. 'Carry on with your investigations in the meantime.'

'No fingerprints on the letter, sir. It was posted locally. The address was typed. Nothing unusual in the lettering according to the experts. Could be any common old-style typewriter,' said Robin, a few days later.

I asked, 'Any results from the newspaper advert?'

'Nothing yet, sir. Still, early days,' Mary replied.

'Can't help wondering why the writer has suddenly got a conscience about this,' I said. 'He could have been holding this info for twenty years. So, why now?'

Mary suggested, 'I wonder, sir, if Inspector, er, Mr Denison could show any light on this. Worth a try, I think.'

'Yes, maybe. He might recall something. I'll give him a ring. Thanks, Mary.' I lifted the phone.

'Hi, Walter, Jacob here. Just a little query: do you recall ever getting a letter, in cutout lettering, involving Malone and Co. We just got one from a man, or woman, claiming to have been involved with the killings twenty years ago.'

Denison replied, 'Hello, Jacob. It does ring a bell. Shortly after the incident, I received a letter saying they, the writer, were haunted with guilt. I was not surprised considering the brutality of the deaths. However, nothing more came of it. There were no clues as to who sent it, no prints, no saliva on the stamp, nothing.'

'This one is the same, except he or she used those new self-adhesive stamps. Actually sent it first-class too. We've had experts examine it. Apart from poor grammar, it has not helped at all.'

'Poor grammar? That sounds familiar. The old one was a nightmare of spelling mistakes. Would you mind if I come in and take a look?'

'Yes, sure, Walter,' I said.

An hour later, he was in my office. I said, 'I got the old records of the six murders from storage and found the original letter.' I handed it over to Walter.

'By gum, that takes me back,' Denison said. He compared the two letters. 'Yes, the same spelling errors. I would say it is the same person without a doubt. See the introduction, "TO WHO IT MITE CONCERN". And using "GEEZER" and misspelling "HARVIE". No doubt about it.'

'That's what I thought too,' I said. 'The envelope typed on the same machine, it looks like.'

'We put an advert in the paper to try to get a response, but nothing.'

'The letters seem to be from the same magazine. Have they looked at which magazine?' Denison asked.

'Yes, they think it is *Model Soldier Monthly*,' I replied.

Denison said, 'So, a long-term subscriber to that magazine. He is probably a keen model maker. One of the miniature battle fanatics. They travel around to venues and fight battles with Napoleonic or Roman soldiers and such. I used to collect a few, myself, back in the day. Got bored after a few months, though. Think they are up in the loft.'

'I think you have hit the nail on the head. We can check local newsagents for regular subscribers to *Model Soldier Monthly* and he is bound to be on a list.' I shouted for Robin to join us.

'Robin, I have a job for you. Walter has pointed out that the anonymous letter writer is probably a model fanatic. Model soldiers to be exact. I want you to go around all the newsagents and compile a list of all subscribers to *Model Soldier Monthly*.'

'Yes, sir. I'll get on it right away.—Hello, Mr Denison, nice to see you again, sir.' He then addressed me, 'Can I get Kelvin or Mary to help, sir?'

'Yes, of course, if one of them is free.' Robin hurried away.

'Good lad that Robin,' Denison commented. 'Got his head screwed on, he has, He'll be after your job soon, Jacob.' He laughed. 'No doubt about it.'

'Not for a few years, I hope,' I said and laughed.

Denison added, 'In the meantime, I could have a look at those interviewed after the six murders. I recall there was quite a number. Almost every criminal within a hundred miles.'

'Yes, that sounds like a good idea. Bound to be a few deceased,' I said.

Denison was given a desk and a heap of dusty files from ages past. He was glowing with enthusiasm. *Great to be doing something useful at last,* he thought.

After a few days, Denison came to my office. 'Just finished checking those old files, Jacob. Made interesting reading indeed. I have made a list—about twenty names of possible suspects. Many have died or are in prison so the latter are unlikely to have sent this letter. They all live here in Castlewood, at least going by the last known addresses. I did a quick check of the electoral register and they are still listed.' He handed me the list.

'Hmm, good work, Walter. I'll get the staff to visit them. We'll see if they are model enthusiasts or have a typewriter. We have a list of the magazine readers too.' I compared the two lists. 'There are seven of your twenty who take the model magazine. We'll start with them. What I cannot understand is why he wrote the first letter and then, seemingly, continued in crime,' I said.

'As Smith was driving the crashed car, this person must have been a passenger, so is it possible he was the murderer of Mulgrew?' Denison asked. 'The killer got into the passenger seat, as I recall.'

'Yes, that is a possibility, of course,' I replied. I thought for a moment. 'Or he may have just been waiting in the car. The neighbour said he saw two people in the car. The driver was the one who ran from the house.'

'No,' Denison said, 'I remember James telling me, the neighbour said that the person ran from the house and got into the passenger side.'

'So, Dave Smith is an accomplice. We've got to get him to tell who that other man was,' I said.

Harry Trevelyan and Kelvin Grant started on the visits to the seven people Denison had identified.

'We'll take them in alphabetical order,' said Harry. 'Who's first?'

'Baxter, Philip, sir, lives on the Nottingham Road,' Kelvin replied.

They visited six premises with no result. None of the men had a typewriter and were too old or disabled to be going around killing people.

'This is the last one, sir,' Kelvin said as they reached house number seven. 'Let's hope we strike gold. Sod's Law says it is always the last one.'

I said, 'Yeah, it is usually the case: you trawl through a load of paperwork only to find what you want is on the last page.' They laughed.

They pulled up outside 22, Bachelors Walk near the centre of Castlewood.

'Right, here we go,' said Harry. They walked up to the front door and rang the bell.

'What you want?' demanded the occupier, a rough-looking character with several days' growth on his chin, part of his breakfast on his T-shirt, and smelling of sweat. He peered around the partly opened door.

The cops showed their identification. 'DI Trevelyan and DS Grant. You are Bryan York?' Harry said.

'I might have known! Pigs! Thought I smelled summat,' York replied.

You should talk, Harry thought. 'We are investigating to follow up on a letter received recently.'

York looked shaken. He muttered, 'Suppose you want to come in.' He slouched into a living room. A room not fit for habitation truth be told.

'Yes, an anonymous letter referring to knowledge of several crimes, Mr York,' Harry continued.

'Sit yourselves down. You want some tea?' York said, stalling for time to think.

Harry imagined the state of the kitchen and declined politely. They cleared some papers and magazines off two well-worn armchairs. 'In it, the writer referred to being part of a gang some twenty years ago and to being with a bloke called Smith recently.'

'Er, what makes you think it is me, this writer?' York said.

'For a start, all those model soldiers on your shelves.' One wall was lined with shelves full of military figures from a thousand years of history.

'Me soldiers! They've done no crimes.' He laughed, then started coughing.

'The person we are looking for, Mr York, is a model enthusiast,' Harry said.

'A model enthusiast? Not illegal, is it? I've won prizes for my battlefield tactics, I have.'

'He used a certain magazine to cut out letters to make up his communication. I cannot help noticing some copies of said magazine strewn on your floor.' Up to a dozen lay around the room and on a chair.

'Thousands of people read that magazine. Proves nothing,' York said. He looked flustered.

'May I have a look at one, please? I used to do some Napoleonic models myself, back in the day,' said Harry, bluffing.

York reached over and lifted a magazine off the pile on an armchair. A number of others fell on the floor.

Kelvin took one look and nudged his boss. Under the magazines was a rather old, manual typewriter.

Harry said, 'Do a bit of typing, do you, Mr York?' He nodded towards the chair.

'Oh, er, no not really. Haven't used that in years. Always meant to dump it,' York said.

Harry took his phone out of a pocket and dialled. 'Hello, Trevelyan here. Can you send forensics round immediately to 22, Bachelors Walk…Yes, and backup for a search…Yes, bring a search warrant.' He rang off.

'What you mean search warrant? I have done nothing,' York exclaimed in a panic.

'The envelopes of two letters were typed on an old typewriter, like that one. I would just like to compare them,' Harry said, raising an eyebrow. York sighed and slumped back in his seat.

Two hours later, the forensics team had done a sample of the typewriter's lettering, They were satisfied there was enough similarity to warrant further investigation.

York was placed under arrest and taken to police headquarters.

'For the tape: an interview with Bryan David York. Also present DS Kelvin Grant, former DCS Denison and myself, DCS Jacob Marley.' York made no reaction to my name. He probably had never heard of Charles Dickens.

'I want a solicitor present, and what is he doing here? Former means he is no longer a cop—right?'

'That is correct,' I said. 'Mr Denison is only here as an observer.'

York grunted.

'A duty solicitor will be here presently, Ah, here he is now.' A rather flustered, overweight man entered apologising profusely for being late.

I added his name to the tape record and continued. 'Mr York, the typewriter recovered from your house has been compared to two envelopes sent to the police: one recently, and one twenty years ago. Did you type those envelopes and did you prepare the letters contained therein?'

York consulted the solicitor and then said, 'Yeah, I wrote them. No point denying it, I suppose.'

'Please continue,' I said.

'Twenty years ago, I was involved with a gang, led by Dave Smith. There was eight in all. I cannot remember all of their names. Anyway, at least three are dead.

'We committed a terrible crime for which I felt truly sickened. I only carried the bag of knives and stuff. I never did no cutting. That's why I sent the first letter. I was too scared of Smith finding out if I had told the cops about him, so I did nothing else. I left the gang, pleading illness. I never left the house for nearly six months.

'I did not see Smith again until about four months ago. He cornered me in a pub and forced me to help him bump off that Mulgrew guy. Well, he said he was just going to rough him up. Said he needed a driver.'

'Forced you! How?' I asked.

'He said…he said that a knife with my fingerprints on it would be delivered to the cops. Seems he kept it for just such an occasion. He said that he would deny all if I told them about him. He had a passport with stamps showing he was in Portugal at the time. Forged, I assumed. Anyway, he said I just had to sit in the car and toot the horn if anyone came by. As a warning, like. I had no choice, honest. I was thinking he was just going to beat Mulgrew up. I heard a shot. Turns out he murdered him.'

I asked, 'Do you think there were other persons behind the two sets of killings?'

York thought for a moment. 'Yeah, Smith let slip that two guys who were in prison wanted Mulgrew done in, and I think they were involved in the previous murders too.'

'Do you have names?' I asked hopefully.

'Er, like I said in the letter, Sid Malone and, er, somebody Harvie. Can't remember his other name.'

Denison looked at me with an expression of elation. He had been proved right. His years of hoping for evidence were over.

Chapter 23
The Blame Game

Back in my office, all the squad gathered round.

'We have got them at last,' said Denison. He was ecstatic.

'Let's hope so, Walter, though we will need something concrete to corroborate his evidence.'

'I suppose so,' Denison sighed. 'Something that a fancy lawyer cannot argue against.'

Mary Freeman coughed to get our attention. 'Excuse me, sir, we have already established that Smith was the driver.' Denison and I looked sheepish.

'You are quite right, Mary. I was just waiting for someone to notice,' I said, tongue in cheek. The others laughed.

I decided to interview Dave Smith again to get his reaction to York's statement.

'Well now, Smith, we have rounded up your crony, Bryan York, and he has told all about your crimes: the six informers and Mulgrew,' I said. Smith looked surprised but said nothing.

'You, in collusion with Malone and Harvey, carried out the six barbarous killings and proceeded to kill Mulgrew recently. Have you anything to say?'

He remained silent.

'You are looking at a life sentence, Smith. Your pals will also be back inside for a very long time,' I said.

'You've got it all wrong, copper. It was York who led the gang. The *Duke of York* he called himself. Had very grand ideas, he had.

'There were eight altogether: York, me and six others. I was just the driver. I never did no cutting. It was his idea, the cutting off fingers and stuff. I heard him on the phone to Malone in prison. They had a lot of code words when they discussed the plan to kill those blokes. Called them nephews and cousins needing education and that sort of thing. For education read teaching a lesson the hard way. They would say things like: "Poor old cousin Jack is on his last legs. He will die any day". That was code for kill him.'

I asked, 'What about Fred Mulgrew?'

'Same sort of thing. Mulgrew was called "Uncle Fred", who was ill and needed to be taken care of. That sort of thing. Wasn't long before York was in Fred Mulgrew's house. I sat in the car and could hear the fight. Next thing, there was a shot and York came running out and we sped off, sharpish. I was shaking, I can tell you.'

'Do you expect us to believe—?' I started to say.

'I was just the muggins who drove the car. He had an old knife with my prints on it. He had kept it so I had to do what he asked.'

'So, you claim that York was the gang leader...not you!' I shook my head in disbelief.

'It's the truth. We had to kill those six guys. I'm not saying some didn't enjoy it, but I was sickened. He would not have hesitated to do me in if I had backed out,' Smith said.

'Well, would you be willing to give evidence now, against York, Malone, Harvey and any others involved? It may knock sometime of your sentence.'

'I don't know, considering what happened to Colin Harrison a few weeks ago.' He was shaking.

'We'll leave it at that for the time being. Interview ended.' I switched the recorder off and left.

Interview with Bryan York:

'Well, now,' I said. 'we have some new information as regards yourself, York. We have been informed that you were the gang leader when those six alleged informers were murdered. And that it was you who murdered Fred Mulgrew. Have you anything to say?'

York looked confused. 'Me? Who told you that? I was only the gopher, "go fer this, go fer that". I was the driver and had no choice but to go along with Smith's plans. It was Smith who was the leader. He planned everything. No one dared to back out. He would have slit your throat as soon as blink.' He made a gesture drawing a hand across his neck.

'Well, it seems you and Smith are blaming each other. Where does Malone come into the picture?'

'Sid Malone? He was the one pulling the strings. Him and Harvey. They were both in prison back in the day but controlled it all by phone, I think. I don't know the details, but it was those two who gave the orders.'

'I thought they hated each other,' I said.

'Oh, they did at first, but some bloke visiting them both calmed things down and they became thick as, er, thieves again.'

'Why did you send the two letters?'

'I wanted out, simple as that. I sent the first one hoping you cops would lift Smith and that would be the end of the matter.'

'Or you sent it to take the heat off yourself if or when we caught the lot of you,' Denison said.

'No, no, Mr Denison, like I said I was—what's the word?—coerced into it. Yeah, you did not refuse Smith. He'd slit your gizzard quick as a wink, he would.'

'Well, York, we know for a fact that Dave Smith was driving the car when Mulgrew was killed. Therefore, you were the passenger and it was you who was seen running out of the house. Can you explain that, York?' Denison asked leaning forward and pointing at York.

'Nope, I was driving. I don't understand how you think it was him,' York exclaimed.

'Simply because of a handprint on the driver's side in the crashed car: Smith's handprint minus a finger,' I said.

'Oh, er, we changed places. Yes, that's it, we changed places. Smith said I wasn't going fast enough and he took over. Then the idiot crashed into a lot of trees and stuff.'

'A likely story,' Denison said. 'Come on, just admit it. You murdered Mulgrew and you led the gang twenty years ago. You are facing life behind bars.'

'No! No, it wasn't me,' York wailed.

'Hmm, we'll leave it there for the moment,' I said.

I called the detectives together.

'As you know, Smith and York are both saying the other was the gang leader. What do you, guys think?'

Mary Freeman said, 'It was York who sent the letters. I cannot imagine him doing that if he were the leader. No, I think it was Smith.'

'I agree. Smith is a cunning sort. He would have no problem forcing people to do what he wanted. Especially with threats,' James Kavenagh said.

'Just a thought, sir, the neighbour said that the killer got into the passenger seat outside Mulgrew's house. Right?' Kelvin Grant said.

'Yes,' I said.

'And Smith, the three-finger guy, was driving as he claims and as the handprint in the crashed car proves, then the passenger, the killer, must have been York, sir,' Kelvin said.

'Yes, that's true,' I said. 'But it still does not tie in Malone as being the brains behind the plot.'

Robin Sanderson said, 'Sir, if we lean some more on York, now we are sure he killed Mulgrew, he may spill the beans of Malone and Harvey. I am sure he, York, sent the letters to cover himself in case he was caught.'

'Hmm, could work, Robin. We'll give it a go tomorrow. It's getting late,' I said, looking at the clock. 'Prepare some questions, Robin, and we will force a confession from him. Okay, goodnight everyone.'

The next morning, Denison and I, along with Robin, interviewed York again.

'Well now, York, you have had time to think over your situation, are you ready to admit murdering Mulgrew?' I asked.

'No, I am innocent. I did not kill anyone. It was Smith who did it. It was not me. I was only the driver. I just sat in the car, heard the argument, and heard a shot and Smith ran out of the house shouting for me to get moving. Then we changed places after a few miles, we crashed and had to walk home. It was dark so no one saw us.'

'We do not believe your story for one minute, York,' Denison said.

'Please yourself,' York was defiant.

'You will be in prison for the rest of your life. If you admit your crimes and name Malone and Harvey as your leaders, the judge may be lenient. Come on, it's your only chance to get a reduced sentence,' I said.

'What age are you? Forty? Better a twenty-year stretch rather than life…perhaps forty years,' Denison said.

York looked scared. 'If I did that, I would be as good as dead. They would get me or pay someone to get me. Even in solitary I would not be safe. No, I cannot, I dare not, tell you anything about Malone.'

Robin interrupted. 'York, yesterday a thorough search was made of your property. Guess what was found?'

'I have no idea,' York replied. He was sweating.

'In a cavity dug into a wall was a handgun. It was concealed behind a picture of one of your battle contests, Roman legions. The bullets match those used to kill Mulgrew and the six guys back in the day.'

York slumped down in his seat, defeated. All show of bravado was gone. 'Alright, I suppose I can't argue with that.'

'Malone, Sid Malone, and Harvey paid me to do Mulgrew. They gave me the cash when they got out of prison. You'll find it under a floorboard in the back bedroom. Their fingerprints will be all over them.'

Denison spoke urgently, 'Were they behind the six murders, too?'

York hesitated, then, leaning forward with his head in his hands, said, 'Yes, they ordered it. You don't refuse Sid. He would have got me killed if I had. He's evil. I'm as good as dead now! I need police protection.' He groaned.

Denison said, speaking as calmly as possible, 'If you tell all in court, those two will be securely locked away. You will have to serve your sentence, in a distant prison, but maybe under a false name.' Denison looked at me seeking agreement.

'I don't see why not if the judge approves,' I said. Denison sat back and breathed a sigh of relief.

'Millicent, you'll never guess!' Denison shouted as he came through their front door.

'What about?' she replied from the kitchen.

'We have the pair of them under arrest for all seven murders. They were behind them all!'

'That's wonderful news, Dear. How did you prove it' Millicent asked.

'A bloke named York confessed to killing Mulgrew and being part of the gang twenty years ago. He named Malone and Harvey as the ones behind it all.'

'This calls for a celebration. Where's that bottle of champers we got last Christmas?'

'I have it in the fridge chilling. I knew you would nab those two someday!' Millicent grinned.

'You never cease to amaze me, Mrs Denison.' He gave her a hug and a kiss.

'Oh, go on, get your pipe and put your feet up,' she said, laughing. 'I'll put the kettle on and make some sandwiches. We can have the champagne later. Maybe get a couple more bottles. I'll invite your former staff and Jacob.'

Denison grinned and opened a window.

The cat had the last word, 'Miaow!' and jumped onto his lap.

The End

Other books by this author:

Verdict Unknown
Verdict Unknown...the sequel
The Sheriff of River Bend
Des Pond, Special Agent
Another Adventure for Des Pond

Detective Inspector Denison Stories
(The Imposter and the Imposters' Murders)

3 Bartonshire tales:
The Wartime Adventures of Harry Harris
The Impossible Quest
The Heir...Apparently and Ashes to Ashes

The Spanish Armada...what if it had all gone wrong?

For Children:
The Life and Times of Victoria-Ann Penny
Cats versus Birds or A Bird in the Paw...